Rock Walls
and
Open Pastures
A Quabbin Quills Anthology

Perpetual Imagination
Boston • Northampton • New York

881 Main St #10
Fitchburg, MA 01420

info@perpetualimagination.com

Manufactured in The United States of America.

1 2 3 4 5 6 7 8 9 10

First Edition

ISBN-13: 978-1-7352576-5-5

Library of Congress Control Number in process for this title.

CONTENTS

ROCKY ROADS

GREENER PASTURES

2025 SCHOLARSHIP WINNERS

1ST PLACE WINNER

ECHOES OF THE EARTH
Samantha Carlson

Over the hills and through the rolling stones,
Transportation through the valley, not a whisper shall be known.
A lone tree resides open and alone.
Through the blades of green you have entered the land of time unknown,
Who knew these unwavering green fields could make me feel so
Exposed?
Miles upon miles, steps upon steps—this ancient tale has been lost
to voices untold.
The wind carries stories through the rings of wood made long ago,
My mother and her mother let those stories weave their hair.
They rolled through the sea of green without a care.
The echoes of their laughter now fill the air.
Stepping stones have been crossed
Now I follow the path of the forever-known,
For in atavistic places you are never alone.
Some ancient tales are better off being shown.

2ND PLACE WINNER

FROM WOOL TO WEALTH
Olly Lefsyk

A shepherd, a nomad, an aesthetic voyager. The city waited for him, calling his name, a fortune waiting. He reminded himself of this constantly, for a true calling will never stop calling you. It was time to accept this fate and begin the journey. All he had was himself, his dog, a herd of sheep, a bag of money, and a bag of supplies. Everything else waited for him in the bustling market of the city. He'd sell his sheep, he'd find a home, he'd make a name for himself, he would become a man.

The trek began three days ago. Ciaran packed a thin wool blanket, cheeses, a loaf of bread, preserved cabbage, a few onions and potatoes, and a drawstring bag of all the coins he had. His dog, Maeve, accompanied. She was young, as was he. A good dog, loyal as any other. He felt he had a closer relationship with that dog than anyone else in his village. Most of his days were spent in fields anyway, his sheep grazing and Maeve herding them around. Just the two of them before going home each night. But not now, for he had no home to return to.

He had sold it, he sold just about everything for money to begin his journey. A week, at most. He would travel the plains, sleeping under stars in the warm summer nights. He'd spend those nights dreaming the same dream of his new life.

He'd have a home, not a huge one, but big enough for himself, for Maeve, and visitors. He would find a job, perhaps making shoes, working on a farm, or working simply as a handyman doing odd jobs. Whatever would give him the money he needed to live, for this new life would be simpler.

He walked with Maeve at his side, she panted and trotted along. The herd was ahead of them. Ciaran reached to gently stroke her long and dark fur. Her head lifted, looking back at him. Some say an animal and their owner look alike. He and she did not. His hair grew straight and brown. His eyes were blue, constantly squinting in the sun. She was black with a white chest.

3

The current field they travelled in was adorned with wildflowers of all colors, the sheep grazed between that and the grass. They bleated, not moving much. It seemed like all they did was eat.

Ciaran had no desire to rush the journey for he knew this was his last trip with the sheep. He would sell them all, getting money from each. He would never see them again. The thought of this bothered him. He loved his sheep, he knew each one. He knew the skittish ones, the outgoing, the smaller, the larger, the dominant, the aggressive, the gentle. Each had a personality, like anything else. His hand brushed Maeve, scratching her ears and dragged his hand to her muzzle, and lifted her chin to look at him.

"Just a few more days, girl. Just you and me together after this." He nodded to himself as she whined and moved her head. His hand brushed his hair back from his face, beads of sweat on his forehead. The sun beat down, the fields green, flowers bright. It was stunning, really. Being a shepherd was hard work, traveling the plains all day was exhausting but God, was it beautiful. All day to be in fields, grass and old rock walls that were from ancestors before him, trees lining the pastures they travelled through. His hands stuffed themselves into his pockets.

"You, me, and maybe a fine lady as well. With long hair, and dark eyes." Ciaran added, nodding again and glancing down at Maeve. The boy smiled, more so at his words than the dog herself before petting her again. He snacked on small broken off chunks of cheese, breaking off pieces of a loaf of bread with it. Maeve guided the sheep over a hill, down into the valley below where a stream went through. The sheep drank, Ciaran filled a canteen while Maeve lapped water up loudly beside him. He knelt down beside the water, hands cupping it up before splashing it onto his face. Though the sun was hot, there was a relieving chill in the water that he couldn't resist letting out a long pleased sigh. He was sweating, and Maeve smelled like… well, dog.

"Just you wait, Maeve. We're gonna get a nice house, with a bath. Oh, I can imagine it now. A big fireplace with a hearth, a bed for us by it, a garden, and a real big kitchen. It will be perfect, and it will be all *ours*." He smiled, petting her. The dog's tail wagged. Her tongue hung out the side of her mouth as she panted loudly to cool herself. Ciaran would continue with this group, trying to get to a nice place for the night, more specifically out from the valley to flatter ground.

Evening came, he settled with the sheep in the grass. They all lay bundled together, it was quieter other than soft bleats and rustling of the sheep in the grass.

Ciaran laid back against the soft earth with a sigh, his arms behind his head as he looked up at the sky above, marveling at the thousands of stars twinkling. Some people liked to count sheep to sleep, counting sheep made him anxious. He needed them to all be there, and thankfully they always were. He liked to count stars until he slept. The beauty of the vast, open field and the peaceful serenity made his heart swell with a feeling of contentment. He took a deep breath and exhaled, a hand moving and resting on Maeve's sleeping body beside him.

The flowers and grass mixed with the smell of the earth below him made a sort of earthy, sweet perfume in the air.

"After this we won't sleep in the grass ever again. We'll have a big bed, and a warm fire. No smell of sheep. God, can you imagine it, girl?" He asked Maeve, rolling onto his side to look and speak to her. She just whined again, tired as he.

Ciaran fell asleep, pondering on his dream that seemed just over the horizon. His new life of luxury, riches and wealth. Though he was sure he would miss this, and every few hours on the journey he would wonder if it was what he truly even wanted. It was, he knew that. He didn't have money now. Not enough. It wasn't comfortable. It's hard to get money simply selling wool, enough of it to etch out a living.

The sun woke him, the heat on his face and sudden bleating of sheep and Maeve barking at them to keep them together. Ciaran sat up with a tired groan and a slightly achy body. After stretching and squeezing his eyes shut, the day was waiting to be slain. Up he got and on he went. All day, sheep grazing and him talking to Maeve the whole time. He thought of it as being something to keep himself sane, having someone–or thing–to talk to, even if that was just a dog. Although Maeve wasn't just any dog, she was *his* dog, his best friend, his loyalist.

Again and again, he'd ramble on about his dream to her. It was like he'd kissed the Blarney Stone and now would not stop talking. All he seemed to do was talk.

"We'll be rich."

"We'll have this, we'll have that!"

"A pretty woman."

Blah, blah, blah. It certainly was a way to pass time. Though, his talking began to die down as his focus switched to something else. The sky. Dark, tall, purple clouds in the distance slowly rolling in. That did not look good. Ciaran sighed to himself, watching them move to get an idea of how long they may have before the storm would hit. A half hour, maybe? He needed to find where to shelter, of course not wanting him and his herd in the middle of a field in a thunderstorm. So, a shelter he found. Sort of. An area in the woods off of the sides of the fields, where thick trees covered the canopy above. All he could hope was that it was enough to keep them at least partially out of the rain.

Maeve gathered the sheep up and Ciaran tied a long rope around trees to make a circle for them to stay in. He sat by the herd, Maeve curled up beside him with her head on his legs. He gently scratched her head. The wind began to pick up, rustling the leaves of the trees above. The air felt heavier, and then rain began to fall and thunder cracked. The sheep all laid, bleating. Maeve kept whimpering and Ciaran comfortingly stroked her head. Even he would jump a bit at the sudden cracks of thunder. The rain pelted the trees, but the leaves offered some protection. It was better than nothing at least. Honestly, to Ciaran, storms were beautiful. All of nature was. He would watch how the sky got darker, the smell of the air changed, the way the wind would make the grass and flowers sway in the fields. It brought some sort of awe to him.

"This isn't so bad, isn't it girl? We've been through worse." He shrugged, speaking to her. His head rested back against the tree he sat by. He watched the sheep, watched the storm, watched Maeve.

The worst came by, heavier rain and louder thunder. Maeve barked at it, but Ciaran began to snack once more on cheese and bread, offering bits to his companion. The sky slowly began to get lighter, the thunder sounded much more distant. The clouds broke again, beams of sun shining through with a golden cast onto the wet field below, the rain drops glimmered on the grass. It all shimmered, warmth filled the air again.

Ciaran took a long breath with a smile, letting his sheep out of the circle again. He stepped out into the field. There was a large rainbow painted across the sky, red, orange, yellow, green, blue, purple. His hands moved to his hips, a smile and disbelieving laugh coming from his throat.

"Look at that, girl!" He called to his dog who was soon at his side, her tail wagging. He knelt down and with both hands pet all over her face. "You see that? That's a sign, a good omen for what's waiting for us in that city…" Maeve barked and her tail wagged harder in agreement. A spark of optimism rang through him once more, for his next journey had only just begun and was waiting for him at those city gates.

3RD PLACE WINNER

OUR TIMELY PASTURE IS IN A STANDSTILL
Anthony Salomone

When you cross the boundary,
the choice has been made as the future is no longer our dream

You've left it all behind
Are you satisfied, will you be fulfilled
Do you even know why I am inquiring
Or have I crossed a boundary

When you were there were you silent
When you were there did you yearn
When you were there could you run
When you were there knowledge you bestowed
When you cross the boundary,
the choice has been made as the future is no longer our dream

Every sensation is one
You have no need to hide
We live eternally in the memory of a dying light
May I reassure you with some hope
When you cross the boundary,
the choice has been made as the future is no longer our dream

I can recall when I was silent I can recall when I yearned
I can recall when I ran
I can recall when you bestowed knowledge
When you cross the boundary,
the choice has been made as the future is no longer our dream

We are told nothing lasts forever
Yet there is always a dawn after the fall of dusk
The boundary is the past
The memory is the future
What is left when your eternity is now

HONORABLE MENTION

SOULS LIKE LAND
Christiana Dunn

I stand at the water's edge
Vast not a word too keen to describe it
Unending
Swirling in colors of blues and greens and I look
I wonder what lies beyond the horizon
Is it another young girl
Another being, born to other land
Born to question
Born to stand at the water's edge
Does she too ponder now
Are our eyes connected in a line only the water can see
Only the salty seafoam can tell of
Do we both hear the crash of the waves amongst jagged rocks
whispering our stories to another
Stories of growing up across the ocean
Such different bodies, but same souls
Different lands
Intertwined by the same water
The same vast blue ocean
The same unknown
As I stare now
I wonder if she stares too
Does she know that I am peering back?
Are our minds as one?
Does her hair curl in the same pattern when the water hits it?
Or does it fall straight on her shoulders?
Does her soul yearn for answers to the vastness
To the deep blue that we now stare at?
Or is no one really there at all.
Is the ocean creatures bobbing at sea only staring back
And it will forever be my soul wandering
Hoping
Dreaming into the vast world.

HONORABLE MENTION

WHY I WRITE
Ella Figlar

I think our world is far too prone to suicide. I think God should've made it harder to achieve. He should've made it so painful the idea would repulse all the moths gathering around it. He should've repulsed those moths so far to the sun, they'd become burned bright and hungry for their mother's dinner. Perhaps my shoes would be smaller that way. Perhaps I would be born to write about the happier things, like happy marriages and kittens. But the roads are jam-packed with honking and my neighbors hate their dead son. There's a white patch on my blue wall because my dad punched a hole and I have approximately three dead cats looking up at me with disappointment. Goddamnit, I think our world is too mean.

Ms. Vitti, in the wake of my third year of grade school, was a real big meanie. Her hair was curly and grey, but she was balding. She took away recess because Tyrell stole Brenna's fidget spinner. She got Tyrell suspended for killing the class fish. Her husband was in and out of the army and young. And she hated ROBLOX. I hated *her* more.

On the days we were taught English, she would pull out the book *Number The Stars* and read a chapter to us as we sat criss-cross applesauce on the carpet. My assigned square was orange and the rug was rainbow. The fraction on the board was only half erased. There were leak-stains in the popcorn tile above Brenna. Ms. Vitti had *big* ankles. *Anything* was more fun than listening to her read. She read slower than Madison's loose hair bead. Slower than Madison during the Pacer test. However no one else seemed to notice.

After reading time was writing time, and this month our assignment everyday was to type along in our stories. We could choose any topic, about any one thing, and write about it however we liked. Holy crap, was that more fun than read-aloud time. My story was about a girl named Villy who was so super smart, she skipped seven super grades and got viciously bullied for it.

She was kidnapped by her bullies and forced to do thousands of homework pages, and she did them. She was just smart enough to.

Whatever the reasons she had for reading the sadistic trainwreck and giving me an extra star, I didn't care. I had an extra star, no one else did. Not even *William,* the white boy that had freckles, a baseball, and girls at his feet! What I did care about was when she knelt down by desk, looked into me so close I saw my third grade reflection in her glasses's glare, and told me to keep writing.

Ms. Vitti, I'll keep writing for you as long as you keep telling me to use the bigger words. As long as you reach into my notes app and tell me a great line that'll get hearts and stars during workshop. As long as you fog-rub the grime off your ghostly glasses to get a better look at myopic latest metaphor. Perhaps I'll write a poem and use your first name as the title: Debbye.

Debbye Vitti. Ms. Vitti. Debbye.

I write because you can capture a life in just a few stupid sentences. You can dig a grave without taking the flowers. Take a picture without memorizing the blues. You can write a memory up into realism, look it up and down, and post it on the fridge like your five. I write because I have a blessing to see past mirrors and dry-walled tunnels, and I write for those who couldn't.

THE ROCK WALL
William Belisle

Rocky Roads

OPEN PASTURES

Sharon A Harmon

In daydreams of vibrant greens

Rushing to edges of high cliffs

Sweeping fields of sheep and heather

Spilling for miles to the horizon

And the wind, the wind

Blowing down to the clean

Small houses where sometimes

A warm, soft light appears

In the windows

Somehow filling one with all

That one needs

A SAFE LANDING
Phyllis Chochran

When considering rock walls, I think of obstacles in life. These obstacles cause stress. I long for a quiet place when struggling to find answers. Too often I have trouble overcoming each hurdle.

I still remember living through one experience during our daughter, Susan's lengthy illness and death from a brain tumor at nine years old. For me, life was an uphill battle. On the other hand, Susan, without knowing it, taught me how she faced weeks of endless health issues. She was able to see beyond trying circumstances. When she asked me questions about Heaven, I had no answers.

To this day, I believe Susan had a near-death experience. At the time, I had never heard about anything like this. This happened one day when I walked into her hospital room and found her overly excited. "You know what?" she asked, her eyes aglow.

"What?" *I couldn't imagine what she would tell me.*

"I flew," she said, joyfully.

For a few seconds, I had no idea how to respond. Instead of asking questions, I said, "Little girls don't fly."

My words did not deter Susan from telling every nurse, doctor or person within hearing distance these same words. "I flew!" she'd say, eagerly sharing her news.

Some simply said, "Oh," and continued care-giving.

In mid-afternoon, a young, enthusiastic physical therapist hurried to Susan's bedside. "Susan, I'm back to exercise your legs," she said.

My little girl seemed to know this woman. They chatted for a while. In the midst of therapy, Susan told her, "I flew."

"Wow!" The young woman responded, "Just like Peter Pan."

"Yes." Susan seemed overjoyed. Someone finally believed her. *If only I had been more sensitive ...*

She hardly mentioned these words again for months while recuperating from major surgery and learning to walk again. Although her right side remained impaired, this never stopped her from inviting friends to visit.

One afternoon, surrounded by a group of friends and siblings playing a board game in the living room, Susan stood, walked into the kitchen and announced, "I want to go back and fly again."

This time I understood how important it was for me to accept her words. "But, Suzy, you don't want to leave Mommy, Daddy, Michael, Kristen and Pal, our dog."

"Yes, I do," she answered.

"We would miss you," I said.

"Okay," she said, and returned to her company.

What was that about? Did she have a choice to make the decision? Was this flying real to her?

After several months, two operations, and learning to walk again, she lost her eyesight. Before long she was paralyzed and bedridden. Still she insisted on friends visiting, and she was always happy, even singing from her bed. She accepted these obstacles she encountered as though she was living in a spiritual place, never asking why or when she could go back to school.

Watching television one afternoon with her, she asked, "You know what?"

"What?"

"I had a pair of wings once but they broke. They were orange. I'm getting a new pair real soon. This time they will be yellow."

This time I heard her message loud and clear, but I did not know about a broken wing. *When the wings broke, did she have an encounter with God and fall back into bed?*

Tears welled up and seeped from my eyes. I had never cried in front of my daughter. Susan was blind so I expected she could not see me turn my head from her or see my tears.

Somehow, she sensed my overwhelming fear of her possibly dying. Next, she said, "Come here, my poor mommy."

I leaned toward her as she reached with her one useful arm and flung it around my neck. "It's okay," she said, comforting me. "Don't be afraid."

Here I rested in her arm, my head against my little girl's chest. Within days, she was gone. She had managed to overcome all her obstacles. I believe she flew with yellow wings this time and landed safely in Heaven while angels sang.

Her words and example helped me through rocky walls of grief. Along the way I faced many obstacles. Then I thought of Susan in bare feet, running through green pastures and doing cart wheels. I learned to live more fully and enjoy God's gifts each day.

GAME, SET, AND MATCH
Carlene M Gadapee
After Robert Frost

Just another kind of outdoor game, two players,

each to a side, and one objective—

to win. But no, it's not a game. In other games,

there must be winners and losers, but we both

have interest in keeping this wall intact, elves

or frost heaves be damned. The wall has a mind

of its own, it seems, a committed combatant

in league with gravity and the dark. My neighbor

and I, thrown together in this yearly battle, play

a simple game to keep the world aright:

Good fences make good neighbors, but it's not

the barrier alone that brings a sense of goodness.

For a time, we choose to face a common foe.

We emerge victorious, placing stone on stone.

19

THE SMELL OF SUCCESS
MJ LaCroix

The pony, with her dark mane blowing horizontal in the wind, galloped down the road and up the driveway, her pink and purple cart in tow. Her passenger had lost the reins and all control. Swearing, but with a crazed smile on his face, he hung on for dear life.

She couldn't have been more than three feet tall at the withers. The neighborhood referred to her as "Cathy, the Pony" so as not to be confused with "Cathy, the Sister" or "Cathy, the Friend" when speaking about the fuzzy anomaly that moseyed around the hood, grazing on lawns. No one minded except when an occasional garden got trampled. Local children would seek her out just to get close and give a pat. Some were allowed to sit on her back while she grazed.

Her owner, the passenger, had visited the local tavern for far too long. He might have been expecting a little too much from the petite *Uber* driver.

"Home. Go home!" he slurred, pointing a limp finger toward the back pasture, as if he was in control.

Cathy determinedly hit the sidewalk curb, bumping over rocks, and tree roots, with one or both wheels jostling her passenger around as she barreled on.

Was she trying to dump him?

The cart squarely hit the side of a tree, gouging the birch. The unbalanced rider held on as the cart rounded the corner and headed toward the paddock.

Cathy and the cart had come to an abrupt stop. The wild ride was over. Her head was high, and nostrils flaring. The steam rose from her body.

The perturbed pony pawed the ground. Then, slowly, she walked the cart forward, revealing her passenger sprawled on the ground.

He got up from the manure pile, brushed himself off.

"And let that be a lesson to you..." he muttered.

Then promptly tripped over the fresh tire rut, teetered, and fell face-first again.

THE SMELL OF SUCCESS
MJ LaCroix

ROCK SOLID PHILOSOPHER
Michael Young

Billy was a country philosopher,
A Berkshires' artist in bluestone
Who could compose a line of
Poetry in a rock wall.

He could lay up a vein
That ran diagonally among
Horizontal masonry,
All without mortar.

The trick was choosing the
Right shape that would lock in,
Placed just so,
Letting gravity be the glue.

Billy was a bar room musician, too,
Who lost two front teeth in a fight.
Said he lost them chewing rocks,
Said, "It don't amount to a fart!"

He wasn't much for words,
But when he had something to say,
It was as solid as his wall,
Verbal gravitas.

His wiry body belied a quick wit.
His mind could grasp subjects as
Weighty as stone building blocks,
Placed with precision.

He and his partner worked with
Lever, with incline plane,
With block and tackle.
Simple machines worked best.

Communication was difficult
Over the roar of a tractor.
Couldn't hear one another.
That's the way people got hurt!

Last time I saw Billy was at the liquor store.
We had finished the job.
My marriage was on the rocks.
He asked me how I was "doin'.

"Oh Billy, my wife left me!"
No pity he offered, just rock solid
support. He observed laconically,
"They do that!"

Life can be tough.
Grief and loss are real.
If you want to build a foundation,
Find the next stone, and the next.
Move on.

STONE AGE NOIR
Steven Michaels

It was the middle of the night when the screams of Oogruh came whirling on the wind, mixing with the wolves already baying at the moon in the midst of their hunt. Unga had been fast asleep, although in his mind he seemed awake and being pursued by a sabertooth, which was a recurring theme in his nightly visions. In fact, when he heard the screams of Oogruh, he thought they were coming from his mouth and soon, he too was matching Oogruh in both pitch, volume, and terror. Once Unga realized he was in his cave and it was only Oogruh coming to him in terror, did Unga stop screaming. He swatted at Oogruh and grunted. He pushed her towards the cave entrance and tried to turn over and go back to sleep. But Oogruh refused to leave the cave. Instead, she wailed again and beat Unga several times. Only through a series of grunts punctuated by pulling and dragging him did Unga finally begin to understand that Oogruh needed his help.

He followed her to the spot outside the cave where Oogruh and her mate Thag slept together nightly. She gestured to the ground. Unga looked to see Thag lying there. His arms and legs were positioned in a manner he did not recognize. His skin was blackened as if he had been covered in dirt or dust or painted with the juice of a rather dark berry. Wispy clouds of something he had seen coming from the forest when the rain refused to come were wafting about him. Then Unga smelled it. The smell that often came with the elders who went to sleep to never wake, or the injured whose red liquid ran out from their bodies. Or the young that emerged from their females without wailing and got tossed to the far end of the cave, or relentlessly smothered in a sad female's arms.

Unga absentmindedly stroked Oogruh's hair, but could not turn away from Thag. Thag was not old, nor did Unga think he had known him to be badly injured. Thag was the strongest of the clan with whom Unga and Oogruh hunted and gathered. Also, the red liquid was nowhere to be found. But his arms and legs appeared strange. Unga pointed to the top of the cave, gestured to Thag, pretended to climb, then hooted in several tones. Oogruh shook her head, which told Unga, Thag had not been climbing on top of the cave; Thag had not fallen as Unga was suggesting. As such, Unga sat down by Thag's body and looked confused. He shrugged, but not in an uncaring way. No. Unga was perplexed by what had happened to Thag, and he decided he would find out exactly what had happened.

He tapped Oogruh on her shoulder, gestured more to Thag, touched the blackened skin, and waved away the wispy gray clouds.. He looked inquisitively at her, hoping she would gesture back something useful. Oogruh looked at Thag's blackened skin. She hesitated in her approach to the body, shaking as she did so; then finally she touched it. The black smeared off his cheek and onto her finger. She held it up to Unga whose finger was also blackened by the touch. Rubbing their fingers together, the black seemed to go away. Then Oogruh screamed, not in terror, but in anger.

She grunted and yelped in various tones, all while dragging Unga with her. It was still night, but her sounds had started to wake the others in the clan. Soon there were many faces under the moonlit sky, shouting back in concern, frustration, anger, and confusion. Oogruh brought Unga over to the cave of Gugunga. Unga's eyes widened as he realized why Oogruh had done so. Gugunga stood in his cave, scowling at the noise that had awoken him. He tried to hush Oogruh because his mate Eegla slept on, clutching their newborn.

He grunted at them, urging them to go away and be quiet. Oogruh shoved him in anger. Gugunga made ready to slap her, but Unga grabbed his arm, then made a soft clicking sound with his tongue. Gugunga looked into Unga's eyes and saw his feelings. Unga beckoned him to follow them to Thag.

Others had found the body now. Thenmore of the clan were coming to the cave as they watched Unga, Oogruh, and Gugunga make their way to the body. Oogruh wailed again and waved her hands in anger at Gugunga. Gugunga waved his hands back in protest. When he did Unga saw the black on his fingertips; black like the dust colored paint on Thag's body, smeared by Unga's fingers.

Unga's mouth dropped open. Why were Gugunga's hands black like that? Oogruh was now hitting Gugunga in the chest and crying. She looked ready to kill Gugunga because Oogruh seemed certain that Gugunga had killed Thag. Unga broke them apart. Others, seeing this, also tried to break it up. Many tried to beat back Oogruh because they had only known Gugunga to kill deer or bear, not fellow clan members. But Oogruh was too sad and angry to stop now, so everyone tried to hold her still. Unga stood between them; he, too, did not think Gugunga would kill Thag, but he kept looking at those blackened hands.

So Unga gently took Gugunga's hands and pointed to Thag's similarly darkened skin. Gungunga shook his head in confusion, then realized something. He grunted and gestured to everyone to follow him. They returned to the mouth of his cave, and on the ground was a tiny red light. Fading. All around it were other tiny red lights and wispy clouds surrounding Thag's body. Oogruh saw this and became enraged again, but the others subdued her as Unga stepped closer. He poked at the dust and tiny lights. They were warm but fading. Gungunga groaned softly, "fie yah." Then grunted and kicked the dirt over. The tiny lights all winked out. Then he showed them his hands and feet, all blackened by the dust. Unga became more confused than ever, but something inside him now told him that Gugunga and this "fie ya" were not the reason for Thag's death.

Light of the dawn began to brighten over the area. But only haphazardly as there were many clouds in the sky. The entire clan now gathered around Thag. Unga stood over the body. Gugunga, absolved of his part in the mystery, kept everyone back as Unga investigated the scene of death. Others watched as Unga cautiously touched Thag's contorted limbs, which Unga still thought most strange. As the hidden sun illuminated the site around them, Unga's investigation turned to the spaces around Thag. There were many rocks. Some were hewn in round and disc-like fashion. Soon, Unga noticed Topa's disfigured foot. He remembered how Topa had been cutting these large stones and how they moved. Topa had been distracted while cutting, and soon the stone rolled over his foot. His toes curled and jut out similar to Thag's distorted limbs.

Unga approached Topa and pointed to his foot. Topa nodded sadly, grunted, and pointed to one of the overturned large disc-shaped stones. Then Topa gestured as to how the rock rolled over his foot, and he mimicked the pain he felt when it had first happened. Unga looked at him thoughtfully and then stared down at Thag. He pointed to a very large stone, as big and round as a female ready to birth two newborns. Topa scratched his chin. Then Topa walked from the stone to Thag's body and back again. After a few moments, Topa rolled another stone a little distance away from Thag. It rolled, but it did not hit Thag. Topa tried it again from various angles around the body. Many of the stones missed Thag entirely. Then one rolled over and crushed Thag's forearm. The clan gasped. Topa made ready to roll another, but Unga held up his hands, signifying to Topa to stop what would later be called forensic science.

Unga rubbed his chin and ground his jaw. Then wiped his brow. This was the toughest mystery he had ever faced. Oogruh was still sad.

Although no longer angry, she withdrew and started gathering flowers and stones to lay next to Thag's body.

In time, Eegla had come over in the middle of feeding her newborn. She grunted with Gugunga, who clicked his tongue, indicating that Unga still did not know what happened to Thag, but another click of the tongue assured her that Unga was working hard at figuring it out. Eegla looked at Thag's body. In the morning light, it was becoming more grotesque. His hair was snarled and sticking out in many different directions. His lips receded, and the tongue protruded from between blacked teeth. Eegla remembered how much she had always wanted to lie with Thag, and how jealous she had been of Oogruh, who lay with him nightly and made many loud sounds—sounds much louder than the ones Eegla made with Gugunga. Looking at Thag now, she was relieved: this hideous form was not the Thag she had wanted. Then she smiled at Gugunga and nuzzled the newborn at her breast. But soon the body of Thag drew back her attention and she shuddered. Looking at his misshapen form, Eegla thought of Gongorog, the outsider.

The clan had been visited on occasion by this Gongorog. He was not like them. Although his forehead was much larger, his form and limbs were shorter than theirs. His nose seemed larger too. Because of this hideousness, Eegla despised him. In fact, whenever he approached them, many of the clan threw rocks or beat sticks to drive him off, echoing Eegla's feelings.

Could it be that Thag's sudden ugliness was caused by Gongorog? Eegla began to think so. Thag was so handsome before this, so strong. Gongorog was not handsome, but his arms were strong. Could Gongorog have made Thag ugly like him? What if Gongorog could make all the clan, even her newborn, as ugly as the outsider? Now Thag?

Eegla began to tug desperately on Gugunga's arm. She then pointed at Thag and gestured with her body at the hideous transformation it had undergone. Gugunga nodded sagely. He agreed with her that Thag's change into death was transformative and hideous. Eegla looked frightened. He soothed her. He turned to Unga and shrugged in sadness, hoping Unga had finally discovered the truth. But Unga still looked uncertain. Eegla then began jumping up and down, filled with fear, anger, and now excitement. She pointed again and again at Thag, then hunched her body to shorten her arms and form. She contorted her face to slope her brow. She acted strangely for several seconds, grunted, and then pointed off in the distance. She enacted this repeatedly. Finally, Unga's eyes widened. Eegla was moving and acting like Gongorog, pointing to the place where the outsider often approached them. Desperately, with tremulous arm, she pointed again at Thag. Fear, anger, and distrust burned into her face as her eyes searched the horizon for Gongorog.

Unga pressed his fingers to his forehead. He squinted his eyes and thought: *Thag is dead and his body is deformed. Thag's skin is black from tiny light dust or "fie ya." His limbs and toes are twisted like a round disk flattened them but Topa convinced him that was not the case. Now, Eegla is suggesting Gongorog, the outsider, has done this to Thag. Unga wonder, why though?*

Eegla was fuming with anger now. She continued to act and move like Gongorog, but with more snarling and menace in her eyes. Soon, other members of the clan began imitating her and working themselves into a frenzy, similar to the moments before a big hunt.

Spurred on by his mate as was usual for these poor creatures, Gugunga rapturously began pacing and now readied himself for an upcoming slaughter. He rounded up the youths and other males who were moved by Eegla's suggestion, along with their grief over Thag, who was a leader in the clan.

Unga hesitated to join up with them. It was becoming clear that the men of the clan, along with Eegla, and now Oogruh were preparing to hunt down Gongorog. Unga looked at the evidence around him and was still not convinced that the outsider had anything to do with Thag's death. So as the males beat their chests and grabbed their stone spears, Unga stood puzzling over the body and eventually stared up into the sky.

BOOM.

The sky thundered. It had been many months since the rain had fallen. Heat stretched across the land. It had roared through the sky over several days. Eerily, the streaks of lights from beyond the clouds flashed constantly these days, and yet the clouds themselves refused to yield water. Sometimes the earth too shifted in upheaval; a trembling of the earth led to a trembling of the tribe. All in all, the entire clan mirrored the current climate of heat, thunderous roars, and flashes of rage. Unga grew anxious. He could not ignore what eventually would be considered a bad omen.

The clan went searching for Gorgorog. They growled and grunted while gnashing their teeth, resembling the pack of wolves they had heard the night before. They would find Gorgorog. Unga wanted to stop them. Killing him for killing Thag would be wrong. But who did kill Thag?

Unga looked up to the sky. The clouds clapped together as if to answer him. The clan roared as if urged on by thunder. Lights danced in the clouds some distance away. Gugunga let out a primal scream as he pointed an arm at a figure slouched by a tree standing in an open field. It was Gorgorog, and he was frightened. The sound of thunder increased, as did the many lights that began angrily dancing in the sky. The clan advanced towards Gorgorog, spears extended. The lust of the hunt, in unison, backed by the thunderous clouds; the violence took control of the clan. Unga pushed his way forward and stood between the outsider and his clan. He turned to them and yowled in protest. With a series of gestures and grunts, he implored his brothers and sisters to spare the outsider's life. Gugunga hesitated slightly as the sky kept sparking. He shoved Unga out of the way. But before Gungunha could stab at the outsider, a loud crack followed by a streak of light tore down from the sky. It struck Gorgorog. The blinding light sent Gungunga and the rest hurling back. The sky rumbled as the clan stumbled. They looked to where the outsider had been, and found his twisted body, smeared with black dust, and surrounded by the wispy smoke of the tiny red lights. Gorgorog, the outsider, was as still as Thag now, sprawled out exactly as Thag had been when they found him.

Unga was the first to his feet. He trembled; his realization, sad and sudden. With a quivering arm, he pointed to the sky where many of the tribe suspected there lived a great entity, full of wrath and judgment on their daily lives. Unga breathed out heavily, then softly hooted, as if to say, case closed.

BEYOND THE WALL
Marilynn Carter

Between
  land and sea,
a stairway
  divides the two.

Odiorne Park,
 its open
   sprawling
     grounds
       are connected to a stone wall by
         tiny, stone steps.

They lead the way
 to vibrant blueness.
    Occasional waves dance
      upon its surface,
        spraying salty essence.

Fish frolic
Ships sail afar
Birds soar
waves gently lap
  leaving their watery imprint
    against wall
      messages float upon its surface.

Merging together,
 land and sea
   become One.

BEYOND THE WALLS
Marilynn Carter

THE SPIRIT OF CHRISTMAS PAST
Annette Ermini

Most people are familiar with Charles Dickens's classic story, *A Christmas Carol*. In it, the main character, Ebenezer Scrooge, receives visits from the Ghosts of Christmas Past, Christmas Present, and Christmas Yet to Come. This story is about our own ghostly holiday experience, time traveling with a merry Spirit of Christmas Past.

***

My husband and I purchased and renovated an antique home in a charming, historic New England village. The town has verdant forests and scenic open pastures, and its elevation provides fresh, clean, cool air. As a result, it was a perfect, summer destination for turn-of-the-century society folk hoping to escape the city heat. They travelled by stagecoach to their country estates or stayed at the town's grand inn for fun, festivities, and relaxation.

During this time, our home was renovated by a notable architect who also spent his summers visiting relatives here. In addition to designing several prominent buildings in town, he also transformed our house into an elegant, shingled-style home with many embellishments, including a conservatory, trellises, lattice fencing, and gardens filled with roses, lilacs, and other flowers.

When we purchased the home nearly a century after this fine renovation, it had lost much of its character and needed extensive repairs. The trellises, fencing, and gardens were long gone and replaced with a low, loose rock wall, and the property was weary, mismatched, and worn out from decades of neglect.

As enthusiastic young owners, we envisioned the potential the home would have if lovingly restored, however little did we know of the adventure, time, and effort it would take to make the house "sing" once again.

In the initial years, we devoted all our spare hours, days, and weeks to working on home repairs and updates. As the house began to come together, we often invited people over to visit, wanting to share our joyful home.

During one early Christmas, we hosted a small holiday party. It was a Saturday night, and the house glowed with decorations, poinsettias and greens, festive music, votives, good food, and good cheer.

Suddenly—out of thin air—an overwhelming waft of tropical gardenias filled the main hallway. My husband, a friend, and I all reveled in it together. It was a wonderful, potent, and unique flower that perfumes and cleansers cannot replicate, and it only happened during this one cold, winter weekend. We experienced it, acknowledged it, and breathed it in, and then just as quickly as it came, the fragrance dissipated, never to return.

We believe that by restoring the home to a joyful place, a spirit closely aligned to the house wanted to relive its own joy here—to revisit its"happy place."

It would not surprise me if it were the turn-of-the-century owner, who enjoyed gardenias cultivated by her gardener, whether in the conservatory or in the elaborately landscaped yard. It also may have been a playful riddle on the word "garden," inherent in the word "gardenia." It may of course have been a way of saying hello, as the gardenia's unmistakable scent, being one that would capture anyone's attention, halted us in our tracks during the bustle of the party.

More intriguingly, flowers were known for having specific meanings during the Victorian era, and gardenias symbolized secret love. We had heard through the grapevine that the owner at the time had an affair with her gardener. (*Oh, my dear lady!*) Other meanings are "I'm thinking of you," purity and innocence, new beginnings, peace, and good luck.

Whatever the message or meaning, our Spirit of Christmas Past was a unique and special gift we will always cherish as we celebrate the season of giving. It was a moment when the spirit could celebrate the holiday with us in a place she herself cherished.

It is also possible that we are her "Spirit of Christmas Yet to Come," as we connect and cross paths through the passage of time, and at the place we all love.

INFLORESCENCE
Fred Gerhard

Inspired by the sculpture Queen Anne's Lace *by Gints Grinberg*

"sitting still all summer…the height of my ambition."
—Queen Anne

Tall by feral ferns and stone wall
I flourish in wind—bend and dance—
A leaf extended to wave o'er the expanse
—and yes—I greet thee below
For I am Anne

How much of us is meant for sky
Where petals play and pry
The hydraulics of heaven—
From bitter rain on greening turf
An endless legacy of luminous lace

—I'll tell you a secret
I was once called
Wild Carrot—
Bird's Nest—
Brandy Nan

What wild name remains in you
If you can cast back
To beginnings
Celtic or Beal of Sun—
Rise up and bloom

—I lace the tiny ones' reflected light
Of hope and love—
Casting kind shadows
For dappling dreams
Of inflorescence

—I Unite these
Into one Great Expanse—
Inhale the waves of wilds
You earthy multitude taking hands
Across Queen Anne's dance

What legacy then
—you clusters of flowers
Once I nod from the sky
To you to wake the starry ground
—you must bear The Crown

THE GIRL IN THE GLASS
Chele Pedersen Smith

There she was again, in the third-story window. Mick knew she'd been watching them all week, hiding in the silhouette of long black lace. Who the heck was she? What did she want? She reminded him of Norman Bates's mother in *Psycho*.

He shuddered, staring, and then wham! The winning puck whizzed past him and hit the net, jerking him back to reality. "H. E. double hockey sticks!"

It was lame but fun to say because it fit the sport, but then a clashing symphony of real swears, jeers, and cheers slammed his ears.

"Goal, whoo-hoo!" Wanda danced around, waving her stick horizontally for emphasis. "You rock, Mickster."

"Get your head in the game, Whitman!" This from his older brother, Greg.

The opposing team bladed over, skidding sideways. The shavings fluffed a slushie around Mick's feet.

Dylan slapped his shoulder. "Thanks for the points, man!"

"Twisting cloud balloons in your mind again?" Kyle teased.

"It finally paid off—for us!" Wally snorted.

"Very funny." Mick took his helmet off, shaking his sweaty, blonde hair and giving them his best intimidating glare before they all burst out laughing. It was just a buddy game on the lake, most of them high school seniors goofing off on February break. It was the harshest month in Massachusetts, so no worries about melted spots plunging them under. Somehow, the friends had managed to get together four times this week.

Besides Greg, Mick's teammates were twins, Kelsey and Ray. They glided over.

"What's got you dazed?" Ray glanced in the direction of Mick's trance. "Those kids on sleds? They're a safe distance away."

"No, look! Someone keeps spying on us. I swear, every time we come here to play, she's there." Mick nodded toward a lavender Victorian house across the lake, down the road near the Boy Scout camp.

"Ooh, do the scouts want to steal our sticks for firewood?" Wanda sneered. Raising hers high, she whooped. "Just try and get 'em, boys! I can snap this over your heads like a twig!"

"Shhh, it's not them," Mick began, but a big C-R-A-C-K froze them in their tracks. Would Wanda really damage her sports equipment, or worse? They always feared her loud mouth would cause a fissure. It wouldn't be the first time. Her singing once broke a mirror.

They turned to Wanda and sighed relief. She had only broken a fat pretzel rod in half.

"Chill, girl," Kelsey hushed. "And lay off the energy drinks, will ya?"

"Look, she moved!" Mick pointed. "See that top window shaped like a flower? I think it's a girl. She's been watching us every day."

Kyle glared. "What's her problem?"

"Maybe she's new in town," Kelsey guessed.

They skated closer, all staring hard, trying to make out the details.

Mick was enthralled. "Doesn't she look ghoulish with that black lace?"

"Oooh, Mickey has a crush," Dylan teased. "I hope she works out better than your track record."

Mick wasn't sure if he meant dating or cross-country running.

"Cut it out." Mick nudged. "What if she's an old lady, or... a ghost?"

Greg rolled his eyes. "You watch too many horror movies."

"Maybe she's your Rapunzel." Wally pretended to toss flowing hair over his shoulder, then clasped his hands over his heart. "True love was nearby in a tower all along."

"Probably a hot goth." Ray winked.

Mick shook his head and chuckled, knowing his buddy was just trying to lighten the mood, keeping things normal, not *paranormal.* Ray and Kels had witnessed strange phenomena in the reeds on a runaway canoe trip, and sometimes Ray acted like he didn't believe what they saw.

"Maybe she's just lonely and wants to join us," Kelsey said as they snacked on Funyuns and apple slices.

"Maybe she needs help." Wanda crunched into a pretzel. "What if she's kept captive against her will?"

"Hence, the Rapunzel thing," Wally dangled.

Mick felt drawn to the window girl, like a character in a macabre romcom. "We should go over and check."

Everyone agreed. Leaving their hockey sticks but keeping their snacks, they glided as close as they could up to the bordering snowbank.

Mick craned his neck. "She's still there."

"Look." Kelsey tossed snow on the side of the house. "Metal footholds run up along the wall. One of us should climb it."

Dylan tapped his chin. "Is it strong enough? Maybe it's just there to run cable through it."

"That's trespassing," Kyle reminded them.

Wanda squared her jaw. "Not if someone's in trouble."

"We're just speculating," Ray said. "For all we know, she's just bored."

"Exactly." Mick agreed. "By checking on her, we'll add excitement."

Greg grimaced. "Unless her folks call the cops."

"Cool. You just convinced me." Wanda hopped over into the yard. After yanking off her skates, she cupped her hands and hollered, "If the police show up, say 'hi' to my dad."

Kelsey shook her head. "She's cray-cray."

Everyone agreed, watching Wanda grab rung after rung.

"I'm grateful one of us is." Mick's neck started to spasm as the daredevil ascended.

"It's actually better that a girl is doing this," Kelsey mused.

"Oh, you and your women's lib!" Ray scoffed.

Kels glared. "No. A guy peering in windows? There's a name for that."

"Ahh, right!" Enlightenment dawned on them.

"And a friendly female face is more soothing, less startling," Kelsey assured.

"Wanda's not exactly the welcome wagon committee," Dylan snorted as they all laughed.

Mick held his breath as Wanda made it to the top window, teetering as she peered in.

Ray winced. "You know, we could've just knocked on the front door."

Wally smacked his own forehead. "Yeah, why didn't we just do that?"

"Because we needed to go straight to the source." Mick's eyes were glued to Wanda rubbing the glass pane with her coat sleeve.

"Don't pass Go, skip the two-hundred bucks, and probably land in the slammer," mumbled Kyle, paraphrasing the Monopoly game rules.

Greg nervously looked for red and blue swirling lights. So far, so good. Mick eyed the snow mounds padding the yard. If Wanda fell, would they make for a soft landing?

"RUN!" Wanda's scream rattled their reverie as her thick socks pedaled the rungs in reverse. Everyone scattered, scared out of their minds. While she jumped into the yard and slid down the bank, everyone else had skated across the lake, swift as bats leaving a bell tower.

With heartbeats pounding in their ears, they doubled over, catching their breath.

"What do you think she saw?" Mick gasped.

"I hope it wasn't a dead body," Ray worried.

Greg fished out a Funyun. "Nah, someone probably spotted her."

Wanda slid across the ice, still in socks.

"What the hell was that about?" they chorused.

"Did you get caught?" Ray asked.

Wanda shook her head, taking her time shoving on skates.

Mick paced. "Is the girl okay or not?"

"Sure." Then Wanda chortled like a psychotic clown. "It's just a dressmaker's dummy."

"Then why did you panic for us to run?" Kelsey demanded.

Wanda shrugged. "It's more fun that way."

They pelted her coat with mittens.

"We should've known," Dylan groaned. "Isn't that the house that does sewing alterations?"

"Ugh, dehydration is making us delusional." Greg crumpled his chips bag in disgust. "Good going, Mick."

"No way." Mick's cheeks splotched. *She seemed so real.*

"We better head home," Kelsey suggested. "The sun is setting."

Chuckling at their stupidity, they gathered the gear, everyone ribbing Mick in good spirits. As the herd skated toward their cars, Mick turned to stare at his delusional illusion. *Oh well, the fantasy was fun while it lasted.* Chugging water, he waved to the window and nearly choked. The lace-faced lady waved back!

* * *

The black veil haunted his dreams. Mick awoke several times, then fell back to sleep, surprised when it was noon. He had to get back to the lake. His friends were busy, so he knew they couldn't get another game going, but he needed to see that window again.

"Morning," Mick mumbled, rubbing his eyes as he poured a glass of milk.

"Technically afternoon," snickered his sophomore sister, Sherri, slurping soup. Her best friend, Anna, was at the table. Mick figured she'd spent the night.

"Did the black cloak mystery wear you out?" Greg teased, pulling his gooey grilled cheese sandwich apart.

"Ooh, that sounds interesting. Did you find something to solve?" Sherri's ears always perked up at the word "mystery.'

"Yep!"Mick smiled, and that's when he knew there was hope. He had the dynamic duo right there. Sherri and Anna loved cracking cases; sometimes Sherri's boyfriend, Brad, helped. They'd been racking up an impressive résumé.

Mick plopped into a chair. "Come ice skating with me. I'll show you."

"Don't waste your time," Greg warned. "We've already checked. It's only a mannequin in the attic."

"I'm not so sure." Mick took a drink. "Don't think I'm nutso, but as we were leaving, she waved to me. I still think it's a girl in a black veil."

"Oh come on," Greg waved off. "Wanda looked right inside the room. She said it was a dressmaker's dummy. You probably saw the sun glinting on the glass or a tree branch swaying."

Mick folded his arms. "Don't recall any wind."

Their mother set a plate in front of her youngest son. "If Mickey saw something you didn't see, it doesn't mean he's wrong."

Mick gave his brother a smug smile and tore into his grilled cheese.

Sherri paused her spoon. "You're going by *Wanda*'s word? She accused Brad of cheating on their calculus test last year, when it turned out she copied off him!"

"In middle school, Wanda posted all over social media that I was madly in love with Justin Bieber and he was coming to a party at my house," Anna seethed. "Lies!"

Sherri patted her friend's hand. "OMG, your house was mobbed and all those girls were so mad at you!"

Anna sighed. "And I wasn't even a fan."

While everyone chuckled, Mick realized the girls had a point. "Bro, why were we so quick to believe her?"

Greg shrugged. "Wanda was the only one with the guts to check. It sounded reasonable. Mom, you're a Realtor. Do you know who lives in the lavender Victorian house with the flower-shaped window?"

Their mother took a seat and dug into her soup. "The Taylor family runs a sewing service called *Blooming Notions*. I haven't met them yet, but I have a feeling you will."

* * *

"Should we skate or try the front door?" Sherri squeezed in next to Anna as they clambered into Greg's backseat. Bundled up in thick coats, they looked like bumbling Michelin Tire mascots.

"Let's hit the ice," Mick suggested. "I want to see all the window angles and make sure my eyes weren't playing tricks."

When they arrived at the lake, they laced up and skated to the rear of the house.

Mick studied the window, tilting his head in different directions. "I don't see anyone there now."

"They might be using the dummy," Greg offered.

"How did Wanda see inside in the first place?" Anna peered up, shielding her eyes from the sun.

Mick pointed to the siding. "Metal brackets."

"Hey, this is an ancient house, probably had some renovations. What if Wanda spotted valuables up there?" Sherri asked. "She might be hatching a plan."

"It wouldn't be her first robbery," Anna agreed. "She broke into —"

"Okay, we get it," Greg snapped. "Wanda's an unreliable source."

They all glanced at the glass pane.

"Should we just drive around and knock on the door?" Greg asked. "It would be quicker. I have a paper to write."

Mickey objected. "Let's skate and see if she comes to the window. She appeared midway through each time."

"We'll give this an hour tops," Greg decided.

Gliding freestyle, they jammed to music apps, then paired up for relays. As they wiped sweaty brows and guzzled water, something moved in the window.

"She's there! See?" Mick elbowed Sherri.

They skated closer, all waving this time.

"Definitely looks like a live girl," Sherri mused.

"But what's with the black shroud?" Mick asked. "Do you think she's from a time long ago?"

"That would be chilling." Anna shivered. "She looks like an old creepy doll."

"Maybe Wanda wasn't far off," Greg said. "She could've meant a ventriloquist's dummy."

"Eeww." Sherri wrapped her arms around her puffy coat. "Those puppets are never good omens."

Mick noticed the window girl's arms gesturing. "She's trying to say something,"

Greg sighed. "Charades much? This could take forever."

"She's pointing down." Sherri mimicked the girl's hand movement, then gestured at their group. In case she read lips, Sherri yelled with exaggerated pronunciation, "DO YOU WANT TO COME OVER AND MEET US?"

"Oh no, someone's heading our way," Greg warned. "We're going to get busted for being Peeping Toms, and Thomasinas."

A burly man hobbled down the snowbank.

* * *

"Got a problem with our house?" The man in his seventies stood with folded arms. "I've noticed teens hovering around lately. Prying makes me nervous." Glaring, he ran a hand over his balding head. "We had a break-in last year. Same type of suspects. The copper's all gone, if that's what you're after."

"Oh, it's nothing like that, sir." Greg shook the guy's hand and introduced everyone. "Sorry, we didn't mean to alarm you. We admired the flower-shaped window up there, and my brother Mick's been curious about the girl watching us play hockey all week. Well, maybe concerned is a better word."

"Curious," Mick corrected.

The man's face softened. "That's nice. I'm Pete, Lucy's grandfather. She's been ill for a while, poor girl. Stuck inside most days, she tends to daydream. Lucy thinks windows are a portal to the world." He mimicked jazz hands.

"So, she's real then?" As soon as his eager words escaped, Mick slapped his hand over his mouth.

But Pete laughed. "Of course. What did you think she was, a ghost?"

They bit their lips in silence.

"But why does she wear the black lace?" Anna asked, thankfully reading Mick's mind.

Pete scrunched his forehead. "She doesn't. Lace makes her itch."

Mickey and the group exchanged wary glances. *Was the window watcher someone entirely different?* Baffled chills ran up their arms.

Sherri snapped her fingers. "Oh, it's probably curtains!"

"That makes sense." Mick exhaled, relaxing more than he had all week.

"Could be," Pete mulled. "I don't go up there. Bad knees."

Anna remembered their home business. "Is Lucy a seamstress, too?"

"Yes, she's quite talented. The lace could be for a client," Pete suggested. "Her mother, my daughter Kara, runs the shop. Of course, Lucy might've snooped into my great-grandmother's trunk again. She loves anything in that time period. She's such a curious cat."

"Cat?" Mick echoed. His nerve-endings tingled. *Was Lucy a witch, shape-shifter, old lady, or what?*

Pete's laughter roared. "Sorry, I grew up in the '60s. Cool cat, you dig it?" He chuckled. "Come over. You want to meet her?"

* * *

"Well, this is it!" Sherri squealed as Greg's car rolled into the driveway.

"I love when we wrap up a case," Anna sighed.

"You didn't even do anything," Mick scoffed.

"Yet!" Sherri winked. "Are you excited to settle this, Mick?"

"And see your dream girl," Greg chuckled.

Mick hesitated. "Sure. But it's not romantic. I just want to make sure she's okay."

But was it the truth? He had fun imagining a soulmate from afar. Maybe that's why he didn't go to the door yesterday. Dylan was right; his dating luck wasn't great. And he was gullible. Last year a pretty girl rapped on his bedroom door, asking him out. What were the odds of *that*? Turns out "Debra Suzanne" was just Sherri's friend Terri glitzed up to look older as an experiment and he was the test subject. How dumb could he get?

"Earth to Mick." Sherri opened his front passenger door. "Coming with?"

Back in regular shoes, they clomped along the cobblestone walkway, the scattered snow making it look like sugared gingerbread. Mick jogged over and peeked at the back third-story window. The lace face was still there.

"Guys," Mick whispered. "Maybe it *is* just a mannequin."

Anna put a hand on his shoulder. "You're not chickening out, mister."

"Pete said it was Lucy," Greg reasoned. "Even if that's a dummy, his granddaughter does exist."

Sherri guided her brother back to the front entrance. Greg tapped the scalloped pansy door knocker.

A forty-something woman answered. "Hi, come in. Dad said you'd be stopping by. I'm Kara."

Lucy's mother ushered them into a grand hallway. The glossy flowered tile matched the attic window and their *Blooming Notions* logo. A big room to the right held two sewing machines, doodads, two dressmaker's models, and pretty quilted tapestries. *Hmm, on the first floor, not third,* Mick noticed. The house was cozy and brightly colored. No sign of gothic decor.

"Wow, that's impressive!" Sherri gasped at the sight of a wide spiral staircase. The guests gazed as the dizzying pattern ascended all three floors.

"Thank you." Kara smiled. "We worked hard to restore it. It gives the home some character."

Greg leaned close to Mick's ear. "She might be a princess in a tower after all."

"Lucy will be down in a few minutes. Have a seat in the parlor." Kara gestured toward a cozy room filled with bookshelves. "Help yourselves to tea."

The teens took seats on the velvet upholstery. The girls were drawn to tiny sandwiches on a silver platter.

"Did we time travel?" Anna giggled, biting into a cucumber canapé.

"I know what you mean," Sherri said. "This place seems modernly fancy and old-fashioned at the same time."

Mick was glad the sofa faced the staircase because just then a strange sight and sound floated along the curve of the banister.

* * *

Anna and Sherri sprang from the couch. "Is it really a time machine?" Anna whistled amid the clanks and whirs.

"Definitely looks steampunk." Mick stared at the mechanical contraption spiraling along the gleaming steps.

As it descended closer, they saw a petite girl draped in a pink shawl sitting in the seat. Her mother trailed behind, detaching the wheelchair when it reached the landing. She rolled her daughter next to the sofa.

"Everyone, this is Lucy." Kara regarded the visiting quartet. "I'm sorry. I didn't catch your names."

Sherri, Anna, Mick, and Greg introduced themselves.

Lucy waved shyly. When she leaned forward, a veil of long, black hair hid her features.

Ahh. The caper was cracked! The sleuths shared giddy amusement, but Mick's heart fell. *Farewell, romcom!* The girl was too young.

Kara patted Lucy's shoulder for encouragement, and her daughter spoke.

"I apologize for watching you so rudely." She interlaced her fingers and stared at her lap.

"That's okay," Sherri assured. "We've sort of been watching you, too."

"Not in a bad way," Greg rushed.

"Same," Lucy murmured. "I'm not able to go out much, and I've dreamed about gliding freely on the ice. When I saw your games, I imagined myself through you. My favorite book is *Hans Brinker, or the Silver Skates.*" Her voice trailed off and she shook her head. "It's a silly reason to spy on you."

"No it's not. That's such a good book," Anna gushed. "We read it in sixth grade." She turned to the boys. "The brother and sister want to win a skating race but they only have wooden skates. Their dad is injured and confined…" Anna stopped, realizing the similarities.

Lucy's eyes sparkled. "That's exactly why I relate to it!" She became more animated as she spoke to the girls. "I used to compete, but then I got sick. I've been paralyzed since I was ten. Had a bad case of meningitis that caused nerve damage." She caressed the wheelchair, then peering through her curtain of hair, she glanced at Mick. "I'm sixteen now." Her shyness returned when their eyes met and she smiled, looking away.

Mick's face reddened. Why did she want *him* to know that? *Hmm, maybe she was watching more than hockey all week.* A happy jolt leapt through him.

His siblings' expressions matched Mick's thoughts, and he squirmed.

Sherri sipped tea. "We're so sorry that happened to you, Lucy." The others murmured condolences too.

"Thanks, it was a long time ago," Lucy assured. "It was rough adjusting. I had tantrums, but then I found hobbies to pass the time. I attend school online."

"She amazes us." Kara stroked her daughter's hair.

Grandpa Pete puffed out his chest. "She's taking college courses, too!"

"Wow, you have us beat," Mick laughed.

Anna gestured toward the sewing room. "I hear you're a talented seamstress. I admire anyone who rocks that."

The girl twirled the shawl's fringe and looked at Kara. "I learned from my mother. I always embroidered and such, stitching doll clothes. I expanded from there."

"We're hopeless," Sherri chuckled. "Home Ec was a wreck."

"Stop by anytime," Kara offered. "We'd love to teach you."

"Thanks, we will!" Anna and Sherri chimed.

While the girls gabbed and Greg munched on refreshments, Mick paced the room. Something gnawed at him, something he needed to solve next. Glancing out the parlor window, he willed the lake to give him an answer. After a few minutes, he saw something. He faced their fascinating new friend.

"Lucy, would you like to go skating with us?"

Her face brightened. "Of course! But how…"

"Uh, I don't think that's such a —" Greg began.

"I know a way," Mick assured him. Then he addressed Lucy's mother. "Is it okay, Mrs. Taylor? We can all go."

"Well," her mother agreed. "If she bundles up and it's only for a little while."

* * *

Mick borrowed the wooden sled with the razor-edge runner and pulled it over to the Victorian property, slanting it against the snowbank. Pete and Kara lifted Lucy from her chair while Greg and Mick helped lower her onto the slats. Sherri sat behind Lucy for support as Kara tucked in blankets and Pete fastened bungee cords around their legs.

Anna helped the guys pull the luge toward center ice and Lucy laughed as they zipped around, eventually going faster.

"Wheeee!" Lucy gushed, holding her stomach. "I haven't felt ticklish butterflies in a long time. Can you make the sled do *The Whip*? It was my favorite carnival ride."

They obliged, speeding around imaginary corners, their collective blades slicing floral swirls in the frost.

Lucy's joy was contagious. Kara and Pete watched from the sidelines, a little nervous but glad their girl was finally enjoying the outdoors. After a few more zigzags, Anna and the Whitmans ended the ride at the snowbank.

"With the sled's metal runner, this really is like a giant skate," Lucy marveled. "Thanks for thinking this up."

"You're welcome." Mick blushed. "I'm glad you had fun."

"I was floating on air." Lucy gazed dreamily at the clouds, then at Mick. "I thought I'd never feel that again."

Greg and Pete lifted Lucy and she stood up straight, supported by her mother.

The grateful teenager leaned forward to give Mick a hug, and she wobbled. He swooped in close to meet her embrace. Lifting her up in his arms, Lucy squealed in surprise as he spun her around.

Her mother's eyes widened in worry, but Mick played hockey; he was steady, strong, and confident on his blades.

It began to snow, just enough flurries to add magic. Twirling a figure-eight, Mick held Lucy tight. She kissed his cheek, then leaned her head back, catching snowflakes on her tongue.

As they spun, Lucy fluttered her arms in graceful, flowing movements. "Look, Ma, I'm an ice princess again!"

A WALK AT WASON

Melissa Rossetti Folini

It was October 'cuz the 'crows were out.
A field trip on the way home
to walk across the new bridge of wood she had been the first to trod.

Along the trails there's remnants still
of what came, before the Town.
A wooden post, a random sign
to caution and to guide.

A rope swing speaks of simpler times,
A trash pile yells of now
Take a left round towards the beach
rest on the picnic table.

Take the path on through the trees
but do not trust the map on twisted nails high up in the tree.
A prankster switched the frames for fun
and if you follow true, you'll find the dump.

Over the open bridge, back to the covered one
she leans against the side to say,
"When they cut the ribbon, I was here
and they let me lead the way."

Turning abruptly back to the lot, her hourglass has run out.
The sun was fading into sepia, casting foliage in an amber shroud.
My second oldest friend she was,
just memories of her now.

I won't forget the walk, the bridge,
or the weekly company,
Morrie had his Tuesday talks,
We had Wason on Friday eve.

THE MEADOW MONSTER
Debbie Patryn

I grew up in the 1950s and early 1960s in Wrentham, Massachusetts, a town that is more than 350 years old. We lived on West Street, and like most of the town, our property and that of my grandparents next door were surrounded by old stone walls. I am sure that when the land was first settled in the 1600s, stone walls were used to denote property lines. Those walls are still there 350 years later, although the pastures are long overgrown.

Our house was more than 100 years old and situated near the road. My best friend, Rita, lived just up the road from me. We used to walk along the top of the stone walls that connected the two properties. We spent nearly every day together making fairy houses in the woods, bombarding our brothers with acorns from high up in the trees, and playing hide and seek in the overgrown meadow at the back of the property. In the early summer, the meadow grass was very tall. We could run through it, fall down, and be totally invisible.

One day, Rita and I were playing in the meadow when we heard a strange noise. It sounded like nothing we had heard before. "Oowee, Oowee, Oowee."

We didn't know what it was, but we started imitating it.

First the noise: "Oowee, Oowee, Oowee."

We repeated: "Oowee, Oowee, Oowee."

"OOWEE, OOWEE. OOWEE," came the noise, louder this time and closer.

"OOWEE, OOWEE, OOWEE," we repeated again.

"OOWEE, OOWEE, OOWEE!" The sound was loud and very close.

All of a sudden we saw a huge, headless creature rise out of the meadow and run straight for us! We screamed and ran for the house. The creature was following us, making that loud, scary noise. We were almost back to the house when we looked behind us and saw my cousin Tommy rolling around in the grass at the edge of the meadow. He was the Meadow Monster. He was next door visiting our grandparents when he heard us playing in the meadow. He pulled his black jacket over his head, hid in the grass, and started making that terrifying noise. When Rita and I got close, he jumped up and started chasing us, looking just like a headless monster.

We never did forgive him for that prank, and we were always more wary when playing in that meadow.

ROCK WALL

Julie Veale-McDonald

ROCK PILES

Ed Ahern

When I used to hunt
I parked on a gravel road
and hike in a half mile
on a rusty railroad track.

At a leaning swamp oak
I veered into the woods and
brush burrow over a ridge,
to where two deer trails
meandered across each other.

I set my folding stool
between two large boulders
with a tree obscured view
of the intersection and waited.

The paths cut through
a long-abandoned farmstead.
A toppling chimney and stone fences
were all that remained.

Most of the stones had
found their way
back to earth
but the pattern abided.

The deer never came.
 For several evenings I watched
the light wane on a monument
that carried no recollection.

The aching hand work,
gathering and stacking rocks
to clear a spot to plow
now for abandoned purpose.

I took comforted knowing
that my presence was transient
and when I left
there would be no evidence.

THE ANTEDILUVIANS
Garrett Zecker

There was a new chapter of the book on that night in September. We whispered it like whiskers and in the depths of the safety of our pockets amid the new dangers all around. The lightning. The endless people and cars, some floating down a river that didn't exist the day before, and wouldn't the day after. Water like we have never seen. A godly amount of water that even the cats and the foxes weren't safe from, rushing past faster than a car. Rushing past, carrying cars.

The waters. Rotten waters, refuse, gasoline, building parts and sharp objects washing away so quickly, none of it where it was supposed to be, moving far from here.

It began long after we woke up on a claggy evening. The day was normal, awake in the evening when the security guard walked his route through our home — the big building. We usually hid pretty well. We kept some old blankets I stole in the night from the caged area in the basement shared among the anonymous people that showed up to work and to sell their musty old furniture and clothes. I didn't even know what most of it was. We'd get lucky when new objects came in. There was always something new to inspect and smell. Old things. Wood and furniture much older than us and even older than the people it belonged to. They collected it here, and whenever they moved something or brought something new, we would find interesting things in that furniture.

A cockroach here, a dead rat there; honestly, we felt lucky. Me and my six children. We didn't have much, but this place was our home and was always bustling with new surprises. We could eat like queens. The turnover of materials kept us finding new places to sleep in our massive space.

We've learned. We were always safe in the blankets where we slept during the daytime. Always look when crossing the road, always hide in blankets where no one can find you, there is a lot to eat in the cemetery, behind the pizza place, at the side of the road where someone didn't look before crossing. My aunt unfortunately didn't. This is in our book.

So, the normal day was another day of walking around and examining what was going on in the building where we lived while avoiding people, monitoring to see if anything was dangerous or new. Today, there wasn't. There wasn't anyone there, as a matter of fact. That was unusual as the light went down outside. There were always one or two guards sweeping the building, but this silence was notable. An occasional skritch skritch of a mouse's scurry. Dusk moved in slowly. Rain began to tap against the factory windowpane, and as the humidity in the air increased, so did the volume of the increasing woody scent of the worn-out, ancient furniture. But we were warm. We were close.

There was an owl in the rafters, once. It flew silently over plywood dividers, Hunting mice, and occasionally dropping one and forgetting. The owl only stayed a portion of the season. Someone was concerned. They shooed it into a wooden box and whisked it away somewhere. The mice came back and everything went back to the way it was. Safe again.

Owls always scared us... There was a reason to stay away from owls. They aren't ever what they seem. Their eyes, alien and vicious, calculating. This was in our book.

Night's security sweep began later than ever.

The conical scan of the flashlight across the air was familiar, dust motes picking up the beam seeming solid as a birch trunk. Footsteps made their way across creaking floorboards. We were silent.

A brilliant flash of lightning tore through the massive room, illuminating the raindrops on the windowpanes, spidery webs of fencing dividing up the space, monstrous shadows projected everywhere of glassware, hand tools, plastic blister packs, and cellophane. Everything was terrifying, but at least we were dry and safe.

A massive thunder crack rattled the building. The man dropped his flashlight. It rolled under the fencing and toward us, just inches away. The light was terrible to look at, and I felt frozen for a moment. I jumped up and took my six babies with me around the corner, along the wall, to the other room with the garage where we could safely watch from a distance until the coast was clear. All in a moment.

"Goddamnit," the man said in the dark. Another strange, booming crack rattled the building. Safely hiding behind the wall, I could hear the man rifle in the fabric of his pockets. Another light from a little black box, and he walked over to our blankets, got on all fours, and retrieved his flashlight by reaching under a dresser.

He shut off the second light and got on his knees. The flashlight swept the area. He saw our bedding.

"What?" he said to no one, pointing his light at our blankets. "That smell..." He motioned to investigate further, getting up on his feet, moving closer. He kicked a piece of the wood flooring. His light went to that, revealing several of the boards popped out of the floor. I had never seen the wood above the floor like that. He unsuccessfully tried to fit it back into where it came from, like it belonged in the new, perfectly sized hole. He took the little black box from his pocket and kept the flashlight pointed at the floor boards.

"Hey, it's Jeff... Yeah, so I'm at Tilton Cook and the strangest thing, the floor boards randomly popped out of the floor. Over by the garage. They're right where they were, so ... yeah... Yeah, aside from like a weird nest that a cat pissed in or something it's all good, no one here. This is fishy... Uh huh... Yeah..."

He listened. Another crack. Not thunder; bigger and closer. I lowered to the floor. I felt for my babies in the dark and could see them. Still six.

Another floorboard popped, launching itself into the air, jumping from some unseen tension. It hit the man on his leg.

"Damnit!"

Another pop, and another. The floorboards sprung around him into the air. The floor rumbled. They fell around him like broken branches in the wind.

"Chuck, I gotta get out of here. Something's up. What should I do? Call the fire department?"

More rumble. He started walking toward us.

I had a way out near the garage and it was the only way we were getting out safely. I ran with the kids through the dark. The broken door we always used to get in was closed. Luckily, I saw the bottom of the garage door was crooked, as if it moved up a little or the floor somehow dropped lower. What was happening to the ground? I crawled under and peeked my head out.

Mayhem in another bright flash of lightning and thundering boom. Rain poured down. The shush of the brook that ran beneath the building was louder than ever. I ran across the wet pavement rushing wildly with water that seemed to have nowhere to go. I jumped and slid under a truck to hide. It was always parked there, so I knew the man wouldn't drive off with it. It was somewhat dry, except for little splashes and tinkle of drops ricocheting off the pavement or a puddle. The air was warm. The water frigid.

I watched as the man opened the side garage door and exit. His flashlight highlighted his hands locking the door behind him. Just as he stepped off the concrete platform, the garage building, as if sucked down by a tremendous gravity, creaked, roared, and loudly tumbled down into the rushing ravine below the building in a sweeping gesture of destruction. Bricks fell in a cascade, a waterfall of stone pixels into the rushing waters below.

The man slowly turned around in the rain. He shone his flashlight on the destruction before him. His mouth agape. He was still on the phone.

"I'll tell you what it was. The whole garage and part of the building just fell into the brook... Yes. The building... Into the Monoosnoc, can't you hear what I am saying? There's a bunch of crap just floating away. Can you hear me? Yes! ... Okay, I'll call 911."

I couldn't take my eyes off of the destruction. My home. My kids' home. Gone. We lived there safely. I counted my kids. Five. It wasn't time to mourn or search, it was time to go. Fast.

The man walked toward us, confused.

I had to run.

I ran with the kids away from the waters, hopefully still behind the truck in his field of vision. I couldn't see him, so he couldn't see me. Nature's only guarantee.

But the escape route was blocked, the waters rushing over the pavements. To our right, a building with no entrances, cracks, or broken windows. Completely solid. To our left, the destroyed building and water just rushing, rushing, rushing by. We stood on the only triangle of pavement not washed away or too deep to traverse.

I turned, and there he was. His flashlight on me. The rain drops beat down, sparkling through the light thrown in my direction. I couldn't see at all. I was frozen in the most terrifying moment. Blinded. Deafened in the loud shush of the rain. I lay down, petrified. Dead. Frozen.

"Tammy? Hey. I'm still here at the flea market. Part of the building just fell off. I gotta take care of this, but there is a possum here that's stuck... Yeah, this little guy and its babies won't make it out, I think the water is gonna keep rising and it looks like it came from inside... Mmmm. Okay. Thanks."

He made another call. I couldn't move. I prayed he didn't see me.

Moments later, utter confusion. Lights, sirens, men running around, more parts of the building crumbling into the rushing river. Then, blackness over my eyes. I felt picked up with my babies and laid down in blankets. I shivered. My babies shivered. It was cold and wet. A slam. An engine noise like a car, muffled.

I wanted to hiss and struggle so much. I had the itch to lash out and run, but I didn't even know where we were. Staying dead was the best option for us. Quiet. In the dark. At the mercy of whatever this was.

Perhaps it was the end of everything. What could I do about it?

The engine stopped. The rumbling. More rain sounds, a couple bangs, and we were moving again.

So much to be unsure about. I looked to the book, inside in the dark of my mind throughout all of this, and there was nothing about what we experienced.

More hush of water. A squeak.

We were handled in our blankets again, and when the veil of our terrycloth protection was lifted, I prepared to hiss and protect my babies with what little of my life was left.

But there was a little girl looking in. Blonde, curly hair, and a smile dotted with missing teeth. Way fewer teeth than other humans, and I could tell significantly fewer than we had. She was young. She smiled and covered her mouth. A giggle. Then, I knew they weren't dangerous teeth.

The room was bright. It was hard to see. Hard to adjust.

I felt lowered into more water. Warm. Wet heat feeling of when one of the babies pees in the nest and there is no choice but to sleep and hope it is dry in the morning. Warm wet, everywhere. I crawled to the lip of the basin and watched as a larger woman with the same hair put two, then the remaining three of my babies into the basin with me. The squeak again. The water coming from the shiny tube stopped running.

I could see a wall of water, reflecting the rest of the room above the basin. My front paws held on to the rim, just in case. I looked at my reflection.

I saw my face in the wall waters. I remembered this, still being here, and recorded it in our book. My cuspids. My black eyes and grey and white fur matted with water once chilled to the bone, but now warm. My pink nose. My babies were safe on my back, floating. Hundreds of whiskers, my family. They trusted we would find a place to rehome ourselves under a safer, drier building. No longer a crawlspace for us, but always warm and safe from the cars. Safe from the fox, and the owl, and bobcat like it was near the lake with the spray and the sand and the house and the woods where some others of us lived safely. Safe from the floods, at least. We wouldn't have to search for some likeness of something familiar, because we were here. No longer the rush of the icy floods, but the tinkle and drip of a warm bath. The mother's-tongue lick of a face cloth the woman wiped over me, softly, kindly.

The little girl had a little black box in front of her. She turned it around, and on it I saw the rains outside the big building replayed. I saw me and my babies, hunched over and dead on the pavement in the rain. I saw the woman put a blanket over us, put us in a box with a handle, and put us in a small car. They talked back and forth, and I could see wipers clearing rain from glass. The picture, this scene, cut to the box carried in to another building, into this very room we were in, and opened. I saw us emerge from blankets, and saw the little girl doing again what had already happened moments before.

These pictures were like a memory, but one that we watched happen again on this little box. It immediately started over again.

"No one is going to believe this, isn't she cute?" the older woman said.

"She is the cutest. I want to keep her forever. And the babies."

"We'll have to see, Mags, this is a wild animal. She's had a scary night. For now, we will warm her and her babies up and call in the morning."

"She's safe now, though, Momma."

"That's right, Mags. This video is great. I'm gonna post it. Wow. I can't believe all of this."

She put the little black box down to close her book. I did too. No one has ever heard of our book. It is stored in our collective genetic memory, nocturnal, ever aware of what to do if the flood returns.

WISDOM KEEPERS
Clare Green

Latticed like lace
upon edge of field and forest
Bouldered thick and granite rich
These new England stonewalls
Salute ancient remnants
of memory
Keepers of earth's
Wisdom
Eons of suns
and seasons
Caress
Assemblage of
Hand picked
Rocks
Turning twisting
Finding perfect place
Tickled by squirrels,
foxes, bobcats, minks
Lichen, leaves, sticks
Welcome my
body to rest
Enduring and endless time
Whittle the rocks
Away
As love of land lingers

THE NEW GIRL
Kathy Chencharik

In the month of October, 2019, twelve-year-old Sheila had to leave the city, her friends, and her school, so her parents could move closer to their aging parents. They bought a house in Southville, a small town in north-central Massachusetts where they had both grown up. Now, thanks to the internet, her parents could leave the city behind and work remotely from home. Sheila was amazed at all the rock walls and open pastures they passed on their way to Southville. She had doubts whether or not they'd get any service way out in the boonies, but they did.

The house was on a country road. A river flowed across from them, and a house on their left was uninhabitable and overgrown. On their right, about a quarter mile away, was a small brick house with a long dirt driveway. Next to that house was a cemetery on a hillside, with a large white angel atop it, surrounded by rock walls. Sheila had to admit she did like the cemetery. She'd always had a passion for the paranormal, Halloween, and ghost stories. Her new school was within walking distance. During the week, she'd pass by the cemetery, take a right, and walk up and over a hill to get to school. A few times on her way home from school, she'd noticed a young girl around her age playing outside the house by the cemetery. It was almost Halloween, and when Sheila spotted her again, she turned into the dirt driveway.

"Hi," she said to the little girl as she walked up to the house, "I'm Sheila; what's your name?"

The little girl looked up at her with soulful brown eyes and said, "Mary. But don't get too close; I'm sick."

Sheila took a step back. "Maybe once you're better we could walk to school together."

"I'm homeschooled," Mary said.

"Oh. You know, Halloween's only a few days away. Do you think you'll be better by then?"

Mary shrugged.

"There's going to be a Halloween party at the Town Hall. I'm new here. Is that what you usually do?"

"No," Mary said, "I usually wander the cemetery and scare little kids that come by trick-or-treating."

Sheila laughed. "That sounds a lot more fun than any party. Would you mind if I joined you there on Halloween night? If you feel okay, that is."

"Sure," Mary said. "I'll meet you in the cemetery around seven."

"Okay. I'd better get home now before my mom gets mad and grounds me for Halloween. It was nice to meet you."

* * *

"Do you need a ride to the Halloween party at the Town Hall tonight?" Sheila's mother asked.

"No thanks. I'm going to hang out with my new friend, Mary. We made plans. I'm meeting her at seven."

"I don't remember you mentioning her to me. Does she go to your school?"

"No, she's homeschooled."

"Seems more and more people are homeschooling their kids these days."

"I just hope she feels well enough to meet me."

"She's sick?" her mother asked. "If she is, don't get too close. I don't want you catching anything."

"I won't."

At 6:45, Sheila put on her ghost costume and headed out the door. She walked along the road beneath a bright full moon, which was a good thing, as the road where they lived had no street lights. As Sheila passed by Mary's house, she noticed there weren't any lights on inside. Her parents must have gone out, she thought, or else they didn't want any ghosts or monsters knocking on their door. Sheila entered the cemetery and looked around for Mary. She finally spotted her at the top of the hill near the large angel statue. She waved. Mary waved back and started down the hill. No sooner had they met in the middle than they spotted some little kids walking along the road. Sheila and Mary rushed toward them, making spooky, ghostly noises. The little kids screamed and ran back the way they had come. Sheila laughed so hard tears rolled down her cheeks. As the night wore on, they scared away a few more.

"This was soooo much better than any party," Sheila said. "You know, I looked up this cemetery on the internet. It's on the Massachusetts Register of Haunted Cemeteries. Did you know that? You don't suppose that's because of you scaring little kids on Halloween, do you?"

"Could be," Mary said. "I've been scaring them for a few years. Halloween is my favorite holiday."

"Mine too."

"Follow me, Sheila; there's something I want to show you."

Sheila followed Mary up the hill beneath the bright full moon. When they reached the top near the angel statue, Mary stopped. She pointed to the bottom of the statue and said, "I'd like you to read something."

"Sure," Sheila said, turning to look at Mary. But Mary was gone. "Mary? Where did you go? Are you trying to scare *me* now?"

When Mary didn't answer, Sheila bent down. With the glow of the bright full moon, she read the inscription on the headstone.

Here lies Mary Tate.
She caught the flu, sealing her fate.
On Halloween she passed away.
It was her favorite holiday.
June 6, 2000—Oct 31, 2012

PROOF OF THE ROAD LESS TRAVELED

Heidi Larsen

I took the road less traveled
And fell over a broken tree
That barricaded my pathway.
I stood up,
Dusted myself off
And noticed blood gushing
From my knee.
I looked around.
There was no one to help me.
I blotted the ooze
With an overgrown plant
I found nearby
And hobbled on alone.
The road was bumpy,
Unkept and lonely.
The only souls who
Accompanied me were the
Constant swarming of
Mosquitoes that nipped
At my body.
I twisted my ankle.
Got swatted by an angry branch
And never once saw
The sunshine trickle
Through the trees.
But I traveled the road less traveled.
I can shout that I did so.
I have the scar to prove it.
And did it make all the difference?
I'll tell you this, next time

I will take a friend
And we will travel together
Down the main thoroughfare
Doing 90 MPH
In my diesel truck,
Singing ACDC's Highway to Hell
With smiles on our faces.

WHAT DEBBIE LEARNED
Judith A McIntosh

Debbie stepped out of her car and looked over the New England field, complete with stone walls and a pond at the bottom of a hill. This area used to be a farm, before dairy farming became too much of a burden. The barn still stood, but the house had fallen to ruin and was torn down and hauled away for its parts. People paid a lot of money for parts of old buildings. The town had taken over the pond and created a sandy beach and a place for swimming. The remains of a rock wall ran down the hill to the pond.

By the edge of the pond were her two grandchildren, Joshua and Vicky, and their mother, Katie. Katie wore shorts and sandals and her hair was clipped to the top of her head. She turned to look when Debbie appeared, but she didn't leave her children, who were on the beach. Even with Katie's sunglasses in place, Debbie could see the hard lines around her mouth. Of course, she had reason to be stressed, with a full-time job, two kids and a husband. Though Debbie knew that Katie's husband, Chad, pitched in with the housework. Debbie had raised him right.

Joshua and Vicky were kneeling by the edge of the pond and peering into a bucket that probably held cat litter or ice cream in a former life. Joshua hadn't grown into his long legs and his yellow and black shorts didn't do a thing for him; his hair had auburn highlights, like his mother. Hard to believe he was going to start first grade in the fall. Katie hadn't yet lost her baby fat, so she waddled. She had a mop of black hair, just like her father's family. Though, lately, Debbie had noticed more gray than she liked. Katie waived Debbie down to the pond.

"I've got to go," said Katie. The subtext was that Debbie was seven minutes late. "I'll pick the kids up at five." Katie went back up the hill, climbed into her car, slammed the door, and drove away.

"Gramma, look what I've got." Joshua tipped over the bucket and out hopped a frog that would fill a soup bowl. "It's the biggest one I've ever caught. And watch this." Joshua pushed his finger into the back of the frog. The frog jumped again and made a noise that sounded like "Burr-umph."

"He does that every time I touch him," said Joshua, and did it again to demonstrate.

Vicky came forward and peered into the bucket.

Joshua pushed her back. "Don't do that. It's my frog, I caught him."

Debbie always thought Joshua was a bit pushy, not that she'd ever say that. And she was partial to Victoria Deborah, named after her. But she made it a point to treat each child fairly.

"Let your sister touch the frog," said Debbie. "You need to share."

"Do you want to make the frog make noise?" asked Joshua, as he recaptured it and put it back into the bucket. "It's easy."

"No, but let your sister do it, if she wants to," Debbie had no interest in touching the slimy thing, though Vicky moved forward and made a tentative stab at the frog.

"He didn't say anything," said Vicky. "He doesn't like me."

"You don't know what you're doing," said Joshua. "You're just little. You have to be six years old, like me." He touched the frog again and it made another "Burr-umph."

"I thought we were going swimming," said Debbie. "Maybe it's time to let the frog go back with his family."

"His family's in the pond. We can swim with him." Vicky tried to assert her independence after Joshua's earlier remark.

"I don't want to swim with him. I want to keep him. Maybe take him home." Joshua started toward Debbie's car with the bucket.

"You can't take him home." Debbie stepped in front of Joshua. "He belongs in the pond and he needs to stay there."

"I'll just leave him in the bucket while we swim." Joshua put the bucket in the sand and walked into the water, followed by his sister.

Vicky splashed her brother and he turned around and poured water over her head. Vicky laughed, turned toward the shore, and stopped short. "Frog," she said, pointing into the muddy water.

"There is another frog in there," said Joshua. "Maybe he's looking for his friend and doesn't know he's in the bucket." Joshua looked from the frog in the pond into the bucket and back. "Maybe we should let them be together."

Debbie let out a breath she didn't know she was holding. "That's a good idea. I think he needs to go back into the pond."

Joshua reached down into the bucket and touched the back of the frog again, resulting in another "Burr-umph." Vicky came over and put her finger into the bucket. This time, she got the desired result and she giggled. Joshua put the bucket on its side and the frog hopped out. The frog headed toward the stone wall, not the pond. He stopped at the wall, though he could easily have disappeared between the stones.

"Hey, he's going the wrong way," said Joshua. "He's supposed to go into
the pond."

"I'm going to help him," said Vickey. She went up to the wall and stood beside the frog.

"No, leave him alone." Debbie figured he'd earned some relief from his captors. After a few seconds, the frog turned around and headed toward the pond. He took the long way, around the beach, and disappeared into the cattails.

"All gone," said Vicky.

Joshua rinsed out the bucket and put it down beside Debbie. Debbie thanked him and reinforced that the frog was better off in the pond.

"I know," said Joshua "But mom said I can't have a pet right now." Joshua's eyes got big and he stared at Debbie. "Oh, yeah, I'm supposed to tell you that mom is going to have another baby. So instead of a pet, I'm getting a brother or a sister."

And that's how Debbie learned she was going to be a grandmother for the third time.

SUNSHINE

Elaine Maloney

The time has come to let you go
For there is no stock to rear
Nor seeds to sow,
And while the rivers still do flow
You left this pasture long ago.

With your little claws
You've left your place,
Posts scratched
Dirt churned
Your darling face.

You bask on sun-kissed stone,
I lay by your side
And pay the price
As summer passes by.

The pop of a berry,
That's sweet.
Those bitter undertones
My main treat.

It seems now
All are those undertones.
Boundaries etched alone
Along those rock walls I atone.

The grass goes unkempt,
The weeds wander,
The chilly shade
Drags me under.

The ground is cold,
Hollow without warmth.
The world transforms
Time takes hold.

While you lay
Day turns to night,
Under that weeping sky
I bid goodbye.

The seasons change
The world churns
The grass grows
And you do not return

The pasture of my heart
A keeper is lost
How can it restart?

The seasons will change.
And life will return.
That pop of a berry
I cannot spurn.

For as much as I miss
And I cry
You have left
To greater pastures in the sky.

TREES AND A ROCK WALL
William Doreski

THE WEEKEND
Kathleen Rogers

Terri roused herself when the car stopped.

"Where are we?"she asked sleepily.

"A small grocery store about five miles from the cabin. I thought we'd pick up the groceries on our list. There may not be another store." Ron tried to keep the disappointment he felt from his

voice. They'd planned a long weekend with just themselves to try to revitalize their relationship … to move beyond the "Pass the potatoes." "I've work." "Going to bed early." The weekend had begun with her sleeping most of the five hour drive. "Anything you want to add to the list?"

"Chocolate!"

"At the top," he chuckled. "Along with the wine which is in the back. Want to come in with me and look around?"

"No. I'll stay here and check my phone." Ron stifled a sigh. He'd looked forward to being out of the city in the quiet of the country. Hopefully, this wasn't a preview of their romantic weekend. He was counting on this time alone, away from her friends and their jobs. Terri'd agreed this was what they needed, but she already was distancing herself.

Together they'd selected a cabin nestled in the woods away from others. It's view spanned the village below with the peak of Crag Mountain beyond. From the pictures and description, the interior of the cabin had been completely redone, keeping the older 1880's charm with modern amenities. Ron hoped the caretaker had started the power generator because he was not sure he would know how. *Although,* he thought, *it might be nice to snuggle in front of the fireplace with a room lit by candles. We could even cook over the fireplace!* But even as he thought this, he knew that Terri would never agree.

"How much further?" she asked as he turned slowly onto a dirt road. Checking his GPS, "It says about two miles."

"There's nothing here!"

"That's what we talked about. Remember? Time for just us."

Ron breathed a sigh of relief when he pulled in front of the cabin. In the background he could hear the low hum of the generator. Finding the key beneath the flower pot, they entered together. "Just like the pictures," he said happily. Nodding, she took his hand. "It is nice and cozy … rustic, yet modern. Let's get our things and unpack."

While taking care of the food, he noticed her wandering back and forth around the room.

"Are you looking for something?"

Terri turned toward him, cell in hand. "I can't get any bars!"

"I mentioned that before we reserved the place."

"I don't remember."

"You were probably busy texting." Unable to keep the disappointment...or was it exasperation from his voice, "This was supposed to be our time."

"Reenie's having trouble with Arnold. I have to be there for her." Terri stomped to the sleeping

area and removed her things from the suitcase, hanging some on the open rack and placing the rest in a

drawer.

"No need to unpack mine," Ron said. "We're only here for three days. I can pull what I need out of the suitcase. Let's go for a walk while it's still light. They say there's a pond here somewhere and a great view."

As they walked, Ron took deep breaths of the clean air. "Isn't this wonderful."

"It's quiet."

"Yes, the silence is so peaceful. No sirens and honking horns."

"I meant too quiet. And it's chilly."

"Zip your jacket, and you'll be warmer." Looking around him, "We're missing the vibrant

autumn colors, but perhaps that's good. Then, it would have been much colder." Suddenly, he realized she was no longer beside him.

"Terri! Terri! Where did you go?"

Then, he saw her standing on the edge of a cliff, her right arm extended. Fearful of frightening her, he squelched a warning yell. Hurrying toward her, he took her arm gently pulling her back. "What are you doing? You could have fallen. You wouldn't have survived!"

"I was just trying to get some bars."

"To hell with the bars! That's not what this weekend is about!"

* * *

The next morning, Ron woke to the clatter of dishes in the kitchen. "Good morning. Up early."

"The pancakes are in the oven keeping warm."

"You ate already?"

"I'm going to the store to check my phone."

"I'll come with you. It would be fun to see what the town is like."

"No need." She picked up the car keys and left.

When she'd not returned by noon, he left for a solitary walk. The quiet of the forest brought some relief. Once a bird watcher, he now tried to identify their calls to each other as he followed an old stone wall for at least a mile. It was perhaps three, maybe four feet, high. Stones had been carefully fitted into each other ... no mortar as far as he could see. Ron was sure it had been built a long time ago. He wondered, *How long had it taken to build, and why? What was the builder trying to protect himself from way out here. Animals? Neighbors? Who else would have lived up here?* He stopped when he came upon a breach, with rocks scattered. *Perhaps, a deer trying to get to the other side.* Gathering the fallen stones, Ron knelt down and began the task of trying to reassemble them. He was only able to fit a few of the stones together. *There must have been others,* he thought, *now scattered somewhere through the trees. Perhaps, another animal used them to fortify its home.* He liked that thought. Noticing the sun slowly creeping downward, he reluctantly left his task and headed back to the empty cabin.

Terri arrived as he was setting the table. He was determined not to ask where she'd been all day.

"Just in time. Dinner is ready."

"I'm not hungry. Ate some snack food and a meal at a little diner in town."

"I'd not expected you to be gone so long."

"Well there were more than twenty texts and a call from work and three calls from Reenie.

76

She's really a wreck. Sorry about dinner. We could eat it for lunch before we leave tomorrow. I'm really tired. We'll talk in the morning."

Taking his plate, he ate alone before the fire. He'd been excited to share his discovery with her ... the wonder of the wall remaining all these years, a testament to one man's purpose. His thoughts drifted to the breach. *We all build walls, though not made with stone. Don't we?* He'd seen the walls Terri had built to keep her from remembering their son: her phone, her work, her text 'friends.' *I thought I could make her whole again, but maybe some walls cannot be breached!* It'd taken him two years to realize it. With tears in his eyes, Ron allowed himself to admit what he had known for so long. *It was over! Together, she would never be able to heal. I will always be a reminder of what was.*

He washed the dishes, and still she did not stir. Throwing his razor and toothbrush in his bag, he left. As Ron walked down the dirt path, he felt a growing sense of relief ... a calmness he'd not felt in months. He'd left her a note with the keys, hoping he would find a rental or bus in town. If not, he could always hitch a ride.

STONES
Ruth DeAmicis

The first thing people said about Kendra was how kind she was. Her kindness, her generosity, her friendly nature ... Kendra had it all. A three-season athlete at her tiny high school, everyone knew her, even those who didn't attend Marnett High.

"I think you're beautiful, Kendra, and so smart, and a star! That last goal, no one could catch you!"

Kendra smiled at Johnny Kent as he stood before her, juggling a pair of rocks in his hands, smiling shyly. He was harmless. A local ne'er-do-well who dropped out of Marnett a couple of years ago after hurting his knee playing basketball. He'd never had a real job, just seemed to hang around town, but he never missed a sporting event at school.

"Thanks, Johnny. I nearly fell though, did you see that? I'm just a lucky klutz."

"Oh no, you aren't. You're fabulous! I bet you get scholarships. I bet you get into a really good school."

"I hope so. Look, Johnny, I gotta go, my friends are waiting for me."

"Oh sure, sure. Well, good luck..."

He watched her go, laughing and calling to the two girls waiting for her by a little blue car. She was so pretty.

At the next soccer match, he stopped her again.

"That was a good game, Kendra. We should have won. But hey, a tie isn't bad."

Kendra smiled. "Against Tidewater? I'll take a tie any day. They're really good."

"Do ya wanna get a Coke or something? I'd like to take you for a Coke, Kendra."

"Maybe next time, Johnny. I have to get right home today. Thank you for asking, though."

She walked away and hurried to her car. He watched her go. She left alone, so he supposed she really was going home. And she did say maybe next time. She did say that. He shoved his hands deep in his pockets, toying with the pebbles he found there, and walked away.

She was surrounded by other people after the next game. He couldn't talk to her at all. She didn't even see him as the whole crowd went to the parking lot together and divided up into various cars. He could only watch. Next time. He'd be sure to say hello next time.

Kendra found Johnny waiting near her car in the parking lot of the drug store in Tucker when she left work on Sunday. Tucker was the larger town, with more stores and so on, and it was a good 10 miles from Marnett.

"Johnny! Hello, how did you get here? You don't have a car, do you?"

"Naw, I hitched a ride. Went to the Big Box store first," he held up a bag. "New jeans. Then I remembered you worked here," he grinned.

She knew, she just knew he'd planned this. The timing was too good. He was here just as she was leaving. It was creepy.

"Do, ah, do you need a ride home? Back to Marnett, I mean?"

Johnny beamed. "That'd be great! Want to get a Coke first? My treat!"

"Not tonight. I need to get right home. It's my dad's birthday."

"Oh, ok then. Thanks for the ride, though."

She turned up the radio in the car and sang along with the music, hoping it would discourage any talking. It seemed to work. Johnny fidgeted, but stayed quiet, staring out the windshield. She dropped him off at the school and drove away, watching him watch her in her rearview.

An early snowstorm canceled the home soccer game Wednesday. Practices were relocated to the the gym. No spectators allowed. She didn't tell anyone about how strange Johnny had been, she didn't really think about it. She didn't think it meant much. He was just a dorky guy.

She agreed to work Saturday, swapping with Deidre, who needed Sunday off. Shewas appalled to find Johnny shivering by her car at closing. He wasn't even wearing a coat.

"It's freezing out, Johnny. Why aren't you wearing a coat?"

"I thought you got off at 6. It's nearly 10."

"I know, I worked a different time, and I don't even usually work Saturdays. Why are you here?"

"For you."

His teeth were chattering, and he was rubbing his arms.

"Get in the car. I'll turn on the heat."

They sat in silence, the radio cheerfully chirping. She waited only a minute or two before turning on the heat, hoping the fan blew warm and not cold.

She stared at the dark drugstore.

"Johnny, you could have come into the store to warm up, you know."

"I didn't want to bother you at work. Get you in trouble, you know."

"You wouldn't have. Mr. Wendell would have been ok with it. But Johnny, you need to stop following me around, it isn't a good idea."

"But I like you, Kendra. I really like you."

She backed out of the parking space and headed toward Marnett.

They drove in silence for a few miles, out into the country, on the narrow two-lane highway.

"I appreciate that, Johnny, I do. But you can't keep doing this. I'm sorry, but I need you to stop."

He stared at her. She thought he might start crying, but instead, he suddenly grabbed the steering wheel. She screamed as the car lurched and skid on the pavement, still patchy with the snowfall. The front wheels hit the snowbank at the side of the road. The car flew up and over, landing with a bang, teetering at the top.

Kendra slammed her head into the steering wheel, then contorted back into the backrest with the sudden stop. Johnny still sat rigidly. His eyes focused on Kendra without expression.

He turned, opening his door and stumbling around to her side. Forcing her door open, he unfastened the seatbelt and pulled her out. Down the snowbank and over to the stonewall marking the edge of the forest. He stared down at her. He thought, she is so quiet, so pretty.

Why didn't she like him? He'd always only been nice to her. Told her how good she was, how beautiful, how smart. Smarter than he was, for sure.

But look, now, here they were, and she was hurt. Now he'd probably be getting into trouble. He knew when she woke up, she'd tell people how he'd bothered her. That wasn't a good idea.

He looked around. The stonewall was old and in disrepair. He picked up a stone, nearly as big as his head.

Big as his head! He laughed to himself.

Big as his head ... big as her head, too.

He walked back and stood over Kendra. She hadn't moved from where he'd dragged her. He looked back at the car, still hung up on the snowbank. Well, he'd have to be sure to turn that off...

He looked back. She could tell anyone. She just couldn't. He was sad about it though; she was so pretty.

"Good night, Kendra."

He raised the stone over his head and dropped it.

BACK ROAD SUMMER SWELTER—HAIBUN
Laurie Rosen

Along a sun-baked path, balmy breezes sway
Queen-Anne's lace.
Yellow and lilac swirl across meadows gone wild.
A cluster of cows drink from a stone trough.
Shirtless farmers ride atop tractors,
herd and hurl hay bales,
wipe salty sweat from their eyes.
Feathered branches braid a sultry shade for mid-day walkers.
Gray gauze veils a once bluebird sky.
Manure, sweet hay and ash mingle on the horizon in orange haze—
like the high risk warnings we were once taught to heed.
west coast smoke drifts east
New Englanders gasp for breath—
nature's shrill alarm

Published in Nature of Our Times Dec. 16, 2024

ALL HANDS ON DECK

Sue Moreines

As I raced toward the open door of the light gray helicopter, I imagined my brother Ben watching me as he stood at attention. He was wearing a U.S. Military Service Uniform, complete with shiny black shoes and a black garrison cap. He always wanted to join the Navy and one of his favorite expressions was "all hands on deck."

Ben is different; with many people calling him unusual or even peculiar. His odd behaviors make him stand out in a crowd, especially at school. Even though he's smart, the way he acts sometimes gives the impression he isn't. Ben flaps his hands when he gets excited, is obsessed with anything related to the Navy, and follows a strict daily routine. That's why he spends most of his time at home, playing with the dogs, listening to music, researching topics that interest him, and watching movies like Midway or Battleship.

My brother gets up at the same time each day, eats the same thing for breakfast, walks the dogs, and then sits with me on the porch to wait for the school bus. When that didn't happen this morning, it was immediately clear something was wrong. Ben generally doesn't go anywhere alone, so coming up missing was a serious situation. We had to do what we could to find him as soon as possible.

Dad contacted everyone he knew to help, including The Granite State's search and rescue team. It was going to cost thousands of dollars, but my parents were willing to do everything possible, to include getting "all hands on deck!"

"Hurry up!" yelled the captain, causing the image and my thoughts to vanish. As I reached to climb aboard, he grabbed my arm and easily lifted me and my heavy burden inside. I didn't expect to be sitting in the co-pilot's seat, but that's where the journey began.

The captain smiled and said, "Good morning, I'm Jake. I'm a volunteer pilot on a mission to help find Ben. I was told his sister was riding along with me and I assume that would be you."

"Yes, I'm Teresa, but most people call me Tra," I answered.

"Well then, Tra it is," began Jake. "I was told Ben is 14, of average height and weight and has brown hair and green eyes. Any other characteristics I should know about?"

"Well, he tends to lean forward when he walks, occasionally shrugs his shoulders and sometimes loses his balance. When Ben speaks, he frequently repeats words and often likes to touch things," I answered.

"That's helpful to know. Now, why were you chosen to fly with me?" asked Jake.

"Well, it's pretty simple really," I said. "I know Ben better than anyone and since we live out here in the country, we do a lot of hiking together. My parents believe I might be able to spot places we've been to that might help find him."

"When did you see your brother last?" asked Jake.

I took a deep breath and said, "Yesterday was my 17th birthday, so mom and dad organized a party. There was singing, cake, and of course, presents. After opening my parents' gifts, Ben handed me a small box. He clapped his hands repeatedly, jumped up and down and said "Open it!" over and over. As I removed the lid, a shiny white bead on a blue ribbon rested inside. We were all extremely surprised, since that was the first time Ben had ever given anyone a gift. Where he got it was another matter. I certainly wondered what was going on."

"The first red flag," said Jake.

"Definitely! When the party was over, Mom volunteered to clean up so Ben and I could go for our daily walk. We always followed the same path to start, regardless of where we ended up. However, as soon as we got outside, Ben said he wanted to do something different. That completely freaked me out, because his habits and likes never vary. Only once did Ben try a new flavor of ice cream, but that was only because our dad slipped the spoon into his mouth. Dad learned never to do that again, since Ben's tantrum went on for hours," I added.

"I'm beginning to understand why locating him is a priority with these issues. Then what happened?" asked Jake.

"We walked right by the well-worn path before Ben turned onto an unmarked trail. The entire time he stayed two steps ahead of me and never said a word. I was getting more and more stressed out with every step. We eventually arrived at a section of a stone wall I don't remember ever passing. With his left hand skimming the moss-covered rock, Ben slowed down at a place that seemed to have sand, leaves and sticks wedged between the layers of stone. I had never noticed anything like that before. When he finally stopped moving, I saw him put something into his pocket before looking at me and saying, "whoever gets home first gets the last piece, the last piece of cake." I could barely keep up since I had been shaking and out of breath from the start. Obviously, the cake was his," I said.

"Let's try to find that location, unless you notice something more promising. Oh, by the way, have you ever flown in a helicopter before?" asked Jake, as he made sure I was securely buckled in.

"No, I haven't," I answered.

"There's nothing to worry about. In fact, I think you're going to love it," added Jake, as the rotors began to spin.

We were soon flying and I had the most amazing panoramic view of our neighbors' well-manicured pastures filled with grazing sheep, cows, the occasional herd of deer, and a surprisingly large gang of elk. The tillable land was overflowing with corn ready to harvest, and a grain combine was ready to go at the edge of an immense field. On our side of the rock wall, the land was covered with grass, trees, and wildflowers. Our parents told us the wall was built by farmers in the 1800's to separate farmland and for fencing off livestock. Ben and I were always allowed to roam freely since it was a built-in boundary, which helped keep us from getting lost or straying too far.

"You're so right, Jake! I can't wait to tell Ben all about this," I said excitedly.

Moments later I hollered and pointed, "There! In that direction. I remember walking past a group of white birch and spruce trees."

After gently landing the helicopter, the blades slowly stopped turning. The noise and vibrations that filled the cockpit went still. Jake quickly opened the door and helped me to the ground.

In a more professional voice, Jake said, "Okay, here's our plan. I'm going to follow the path you and Ben took along the rock wall and look for anything that could help lead us to your brother. I noticed you brought binoculars, so I want you to scan the perimeter to check for anything that seems out of the ordinary."

"Before we start, Jake, I just remembered something that might be important for you to know. When my brother comes across something interesting, he'll research the topic for weeks. Then, we hear all about what he learned. Ben won't let anything or anyone stop him until he decides it's time to move on to another subject. This may sound crazy, but maybe Ben's on his own mission," I said.

"Anything's possible. Let's go!" directed Jake.

Besides volunteering to help find people, I wondered about Jake's background as I watched him carefully inspect the stone wall. When he was finished, I thought I saw him put something into his pocket before he turned to walk in my direction. I did my best to check the area for anything that might seem out of place. Of course, I had no idea what I was looking for. I told Jake I had been temporarily blinded by sunlight that bounced between the tree trunks, which made it difficult for me to see clearly. Jake thought that comment was interesting.

"Some of the things both of us noticed may be worth pursuing. I want you to ask your parents to compile a list of all the classes Ben has taken, the types of field trips he's been on, and a print out of anything they can that will tell us what he's been researching over the past few months," Jake stated.

I didn't ask why, but yelled, "Then get us back, Jake. Hurry up!"

Fortunately, my mom has always been meticulous about keeping records about me and my brother, and my dad knows his way around a computer. We were able to collect everything Jake asked for pretty quickly.

Soon after we forwarded Jake the information, he called and said he was on his way to pick us up. Instead of a helicopter, Jake arrived in a dark green Ford Explorer.

"I know where Ben is," said Jake, as I claimed the passenger seat and my parents got into the spacious back row.

"Is he ok?" Mom asked.

"Well, where is he?" questioned Dad.

Jake responded, "Ben is fine, and I'm taking you to him. And Tra, you were right, your brother has been on a mission. When we get there, Ben plans to tell you all about it."

As Jake drove, I couldn't help but think about the struggles Ben faces daily and what it's been like for me. Having a brother with autism has been a challenge. I've always been his only best friend and playmate. Much of my life has revolved around his needs, and I learned to accept it. I often wondered what would happen if my parents died, and I was left to care for him on my own. It never crossed my mind that Ben might leave first, but this situation made me realize I would be lost without him.

"We're just about there," announced Jake, as he pulled up in front of Keene Middle School.

"Well, it is a school day," I whispered.

"Are you telling us Ben has been at school all day?" Dad grumbled.

Jake got out and opened the back door to help my mom step down from the truck. They began walking toward the building, with the two of us following closely behind.

"This had better be good," mumbled my father.

"Something must be going on, Dad. Look at all the cars in the parking lot. Wait, I remember seeing an announcement about a presentation. It must be happening today," I said.

Jake brought us into an empty auditorium through a side door, where we saw Ben pacing back and forth across the stage. His eighth-grade history teacher, Mrs. Kane brought us to the front row and said she knew we would enjoy the show.

When he saw us, Ben stopped and flapped his hands a bit before shuffling towards us. "I'm so glad you're all here! I completely forgot, forgot to tell you I had to get to school early to get ready for this, and made myself ride a very long way on my 3-wheel bike. It wasn't even as bad as I thought! Before I left, I think I put an invitation on the kitchen table," said Ben.

"You mean that red envelope sticking out of your back pocket? I asked.

"Oops," answered Ben, handing it to mom. "At least Jake was able to figure out where I was, and made sure to get all of you here. He also told me about the search party. Sorry, sorry about that."

The main doors to the auditorium opened. Dozens of parents and students filed in. As they took their seats, gentle drumming and rattling could be heard coming from behind the curtain. Mrs. Kane walked to the center of the stage with Ben close behind. While waiting for quiet, Ben did his best to hold still, but couldn't help fidgeting. After a few moments, Mrs. Kane loudly called out "Kwai!" which got everyone's attention.

"Kwai means hello in the Abenaki language, and thank you for joining us," she began. For those of you who don't know me, I'm

Mrs. Kane, a history teacher here at Keene Middle School. One of the subjects in my curriculum focuses on the Abenaki Native American tribe. As many of you may know, our school sits on an Abenaki settlement known as "Tenant Swamp." A number of my students were eager to learn as much as they could about the Abenaki people, and suggested we prepare a presentation that was open to the public. We're looking forward to sharing the history of the Abenaki with you."

Mrs. Kane then pointed to Ben and said, "First, I'd like to introduce Ben Clark, our latest home-grown investigator. He discovered there was once a longhouse on his property and he also found a piece of wampum that the women used to make necklaces."

After the applause died down, Ben rocked his body back and forth and flapped his hands for a few moments before speaking, "When I'm interested in something, I love to learn as much as I can, as much as I can. When Mrs. Kane taught us about the Abenaki people, I wondered if any lived near our house, so I was determined to find out. Every day, my sister Tra and I went for a walk. I kept my plan a secret and as I hunted for clues, Tra picked flowers or looked for four-leaf clovers. One day, one day I noticed a few small pieces of white bark and slivers of what looked like wood in the rock wall. While scraping some into my hand, a small purple bead fell out. I gave the sample to Mrs. Kane the next day. She was able to have it all analyzed. A team of researchers even visited the site and confirmed that the Abenaki lived on our land, the Abenaki lived on our land."

"I can't believe our property was once inhabited by the Abenaki tribe," whispered Ben's father.

Jake leaned toward Tra and said, "My brother wrote a book about New England. I know what it's like having a sibling obsessed with facts. I'm going to like Ben."

The auditorium was then filled with Abenaki music, composed of song, drums, flutes and rattles as a video of a traditional dance was projected across a large screen.

"Now I'd like to introduce Israel Parker, a researcher studying the history of the Abenaki people who lived here in New Hampshire," said Mrs. Kane.

"I'm honored to be here and look forward to telling you about my research over the course of this program. We'll also be displaying some of the artifacts I've collected over the years: wooden baskets, beadwork, and a few hunting spears made from animal bones. I plan to tell a few personal family stories and our connection to the Abenaki people and answer any questions you may have," said Mr. Parker.

As the lights began to dim, he announced, "Let the show begin!"

* * *

When the presentation was over and the applause ended, Ben thanked everyone for coming. He received high fives from students, pats on the back from adults and a noticeable wink from Jake. Mrs. Kane shook Ben's hand and I could see my parents beaming with pride. I never imagined my brother would ever be able to move this far beyond his comfort zone.

Fortunately, Jake was able to secure Ben's bike onto his vehicle, and then drove us all home. This time, Ben rode in the co-pilot's seat, paying special attention to a piece of material hanging from the rearview mirror. As soon as we pulled into our driveway, Ben couldn't help himself and reached up to open it to get a better look. Within seconds he exclaimed, "This is the flag of the Abenaki! Why do you have this, Jake?"

"As I already told your sister, my brother wrote a book about New England. But, I didn't tell her that it also included information about the Abenaki people. That's because my brother and I are descendants of one of the original Abenaki tribe members."

"What an amazing coincidence," said Tra, before quickly asking, "Wait! Is Israel Parker your brother?"

"He is," replied Jake. "And, it just so happens that Mrs. Kane had arranged for him to participate in the presentation long before Ben's disappearance!"

"I've always believed things happen for a reason," began Mom, just before Dad interrupted and said, "And something like this better not ever happen again!"

Our parents could not have been more grateful for Jake's help and warmly thanked him before going into the house to start dinner.

Ben looked at me, and with a big smile on his face said, "Oh, and about taking you on the mystery tour, I thought it would be fun. At least it was for me, it was for me."

"You're so weird Ben," I answered.

"And, I'm sure you wondered what I found," Ben added, as he reached into his pocket. He handed me a blue wampum, grinned and said. "If we keep looking, you might even have enough for a necklace someday."

"That would be really nice," I answered with a smirk.

Jake laughed and said, "By the way, Tra, did you know the name Abenaki is a combination of words? 'Abena' means flickering light, and 'ki' means people. While searching for your brother, is it possible that the sunlight that bounced between the tree trunks happened for a reason?"

All I could do was shrug my shoulders and shake my head while thinking, "And, things keep getting weirder!"

By the end of the conversation, it was very clear Ben and Jake really liked one another and certainly enjoyed teasing me.

Right before he left, Jake handed my brother an arrow-head he found on our mission to find him as well as a signed copy of his brother's book. Then, he stood at attention, saluted and said, "All in a day's work, Ben. Nipskwesw!"

Ben looked at me and said, "Tra, that means good job, good job!"

After giving him the thumbs up, I smiled and said, "Ben, so does Bravo Zulu."

WALKING OVER LOW STONES
Paula Giaquinto

Walking over the low stones

Boulder-bodies buried, unknown to the winds,

Heads heaved up,

Revenant rocks,

Almost invisible in the cold gray light,

Sisters in old walls, now crumbled,

This day, She, too, a sister, stands solid.

Rooted, feet planted more below ground than above.

She stares down the dawn, and

The sun's indelible and fluid swaths across the pasture.

She dreams down through the hoary field,

Crystal pale grass-blades shimmery sisters to the

Granite and mud,

To be mountains, again, She hopes,

In her next life.

She remembers her forebears,

Stonecutters and stone-finders in their new home,

High in the quarry and

Hefting rocks in the low pasture, behind the barn, for

Walls made of breaking backs and blistered palms.

Primitive protection against deer and dangers and demons unknown.

Quiet, arms wrapped against the gray cold,

Ribbons of mist wrap her ankles, tie her to these rocks,

Looking east,

She remembers magic in the new sun, while

Dawn remembers the green push of stalks and vines,

Sap soon flowing through maple and pine, sisters to its seasons,

Wind remembers the red-tailed hawks

Soaring and climbing and circling to heaven,

The Pasture remembers its own cycles,

Its pulse of growing and growing until exhaustion wins,

Rock walls remember hugging ground,

Sometime before a trail head or a headstone grows,

Granite, ground- bound and then released at the top of the hill,

Nearness to the sun the cause of its downfall.

Between a rock wall and a hard wind,

It's hard to tell what She is made of,

Walking, remembering, dreaming, rooted,

Bundled against the cold, the demons, the pulsing,

She is graying towards invisibility.

THE BARRIER
Les Clark

In a kingly manor, the throne and banquet table might be smartly constructed of marble and polished walnut with sparkling blown glass ornaments displayed beneath a vibrant purple runner and whose tassels of spun gold would spiral to the floor. Atop silver chargers, mounds of steaming meat would await knife and fork. Bowls filled with fruit of every color and shape as well as carafes of plum wine would have the attention of loyal servants.

Not here.

This was the forest, and the podium was nothing more than a tree stump covered in flattened white birch bark adorned with moss, home to grey speckled things weaving their way through the fronds. A rough-hewn cup sloshed with spring water. Beneath its surface swam a tadpole overlooked by the donor. Piney McCone, whose nose had the characteristics of a mushroom cap in shape, size and alabaster color, cleared his throat before the throng seated in a grassy clearing on a fan of logs reaching just shy of a stand of oak and maple. The night air was fresh with a woodsy scent wafting through the trees.

When his thunderous nasal honks went ignored, he grasped the owl off his shoulder, avoided its talons, and held it high. Its klaxon squawks hushed the crowd. His nose, round as a dome, flushed an irritated pink.

"I am calling to order the eight hundred and forty-seventh meeting of we elves, imps, gnomes, sprites, pixies...no, I didn't forget you little starbursts...and midges to order. We have much important business to conduct so I shall suspend the reading of the last minutes because they were destroyed in a lightning strike a hundred and six years ago."

Fireflies danced and flitted amongst the audience, hesitating over, and illuminating any unruly speaker who might want to disrupt the proceedings. But, of course, there was one; there was always one. Pumpkin O'Toole sprang into their midst like a geyser, her arms x-ing and y-ing for attention. The tiny bugs spread like a starburst.

"What about that rock wall the humans erected?" Pumpkin asked. "It's a barrier to pasture. We have a dandelion crop to harvest. Wine to produce. I have customers."

"I believe," McCone intoned to the crowd, "that you, Ms. O'Toole, are your best customer." He was an elf of great strength, courage and humor (and yes, he once bested a hungry lynx drooling over his rabbits)

A flight of pixies, hues ebbing and flowing with rainbow colors, danced in the twilight, their tittering tinkling like crystals. McCone raised his arms, muscles rippling from years of wrestling reluctant tree stumps from the earth's grasp.

O'Toole's face, aglow from the meeting's fire, turned redder still.

"Well, I never," she sputtered.

"We all know better," McCone smiled. "Now, who else has something to say?"

A peasant arm waved from the back, his tunic dotted with purple stains.

"The chair recognizes Vine Man McBough." It was one of the forest imps.

"Ye might not know this but when yer harvesting blueberries, yer loses all track of time and I ain't no exception. It's a juicy business but if yer wants them fresh, I best be left alone. I heard there might be mead at this here shebang so I'm here with no knowledge of what's the what. Can ye amplify, McCone?"

Like a zephyr caught twisting throughout the saplings, a whisper whipped up and down, in and out of the rows. "There's mead?" could be heard in every corner.

"Order," McCone cried. "Yes, there'll be mead, but Vine Man wants to know our purpose here. Well, sir, you won't be able to sell your blueberries because a wall of stone has been erected by the pasture folk to keep their sheep from getting lost in the forest where, as you know, things with teeth lie in wait."

"Not with me scythe by me side," Vine Man gestured. Many near him nodded their approval. "What sort of wall are yer shaking in yer boots for?" he shouted.

Like a conductor, McCone waggled his fingers at the pixies. The air sparkled as hundreds spiraled into the air, coalescing into greys and blues, until, silhouetted against the night sky, they formed the appearance of rough-hewn stones in a transparent wall as long as a felled pine. The oohs and aaahhhs hummed like a bow string.

Throck, a tree-dwelling sprite, excitedly twitched his pointy ears in the cool night. He smoothed his green tunic before hopping onto McCone's tree stump, then raised its thin arms for silence. Its voice was but a squeak. McCone, like his previous conversations, had to bend for the tiny man to whisper in his ear.

"What do ye want to say, my little friend?" McCone said kindly, blinking as Throck's peeps and squeals echoed in his ear canal. "Goodness, you're loud." Having made his point, Throck hopped down.

McCone stood tall on his stump. "Listen, my friends. Throck has a gaggle of moles we can use to burrow under the wall. Is there any discussion?"

Barka McCone yanked the hem of his jerkin. She stood beside her husband of three hundred forty-seven years. Piney often and quickly complied with her wants and needs.

"Should you think for a second, husband, that you expect this lady to crawl through tunnels gouged by them little furry things, your gruel will contain what them things leave behind."

Her voice carried all the way to the back and returned with waves of tinny laughter ringing in Piney's ears. "You've made your point, my love."

In the third row, a meaty, rotund elf stood. "The stump recognizes Stoney Brook. What say you, sir?"

"DOWN WITH THE WALL!"

Brook's bellow dislodged leaves as if it were the first frost. A family of squirrels, hoping to fetch some of the night's refreshments of cooked hen-of-the-woods mushrooms, scattered in a bushy cloud.

"Shush, man," Piney McCone admonished. "You'll wake the pasture folk."

The elf turned. "IT'S THEM THAT BUILT IT."

Across acres of grass and wildflowers closed for the night, a corral of sheep, eyes wide with fright, started their bleating cries. One lit candle appeared in a window, then another and another until the family who had been deep in slumber were now rudely awake.

"Was that thunder, Father?"

"I felt the earth move, my husband."

"I need my lantern and pitchfork, wife. You and the children calm the sheep while I see to this...to this...whatever it is." And off he went into the night. Across his field he strode, barely making out the flickering flame ahead, warming the denizens of the forest. The villagers knew of them but when they conducted searches, they were gone.

The farmer, his long strides furrowing his field, cut quickly towards the forest on the other side of his newly built wall. He pinched the candle flame, easing one leg, then the other over the rough stones. Before him, row after row of little people, pixies and sprites thick as a cloud of midges, sat enthralled as a gnome, half the farmer's size, conducted the business of his people.

"Well, what's going on here?" he boomed. "Who scared my flock? And *who* is in charge?"

Piney McCone stood atop his tree stump, still two feet shorter than the stranger, and raised his arms to quiet his audience. They clutched themselves in fear as the giant towered over them. The sprites and pixies flew aloft, forming a colorful protective ball.

"I'm the leader," McCone shouted bravely in the deepest voice he could muster. "We met tonight because there is a wall of stone cutting us off from the fields beyond. We *were* making garlands of the flowers, wine from the dandelions and yes, we *were* milking your sheep for our youngins. We were thriving until someone built that wretched wall."

The farmer thrust his pitchfork into the soft earth. "You can't take if you don't ask," he whispered, hoping his voice would soften the shock of his appearance.

Barka McCone strained her neck. "We can't ask because it's in the way."

Pumpkin O'Toole pushed her way to the front. "I make the best wine from your yellow flowers. I can't no more." Then, as the farmer faced her, she took a tentative step backwards.

Petal, a honey-gathering sprite, buzzed up to the farmer's ear. "Do you know what your sheep's milk and our sweetness make?" she squealed, making him blink.

The farmer suffered minutes of protesting squeaks, screeches and even some tiny tears. He thought for a moment. "When daylight comes, I will solve this problem for you."

By the next afternoon, the farmer's family had not only removed a gnome's arm width of rock but installed a small gate sheep couldn't bridge. To celebrate the solution, a rainbow arch of pixies joined both sides.

The gate required immediate repair when Stoney Brook declared it, "PERFECT!"

POTATO DAZE

Barbara A Reynolds

In folly's field

patched with

scabs of potato

brown regret,

sorrow bends

her russet head,

weeping seeds

of forget…

Reflections of Stone and Wheat

THE FLOWER OF MY LOVE
Ed Londergan

Silent in the meadow stands

A solitary yellow flower

Wavering through times of change

Growing ever so slow

A single sunbeam pierces dark clouds

On a cold and windy day

Spreading the soft dawn's light

My love touches your soul

From year to year

Age to age

Never ceasing to be

Such is my love for you

WADE
Amy L Paul

Pops wished Wade would turn himself around and walk right back down the hill. Wade just wasn't the same now that he'd turned thirteen and received his first cell phone from his mother. Gone were the waves, the "Hey, Pops!", the wide brown eyes that met his own. The kid barely spoke now; he barely looked up from his palm.

Pops turned from the doorframe to the kitchen. Pie'd been cooling long enough.

"Let's us see, Scruff, who Wade is today," Pops said to the old dog lying on the floor in a heap. At the mention of Wade's name, the dog lifted his head, widened his eyes, wagged his tail.

A creak upon a stair announced Wade's arrival as Pops took down two glass plates from the cabinet's top shelf. The sun's first rays made their way over the distant hills and into the kitchen as Pops scooped two slices of the pie and set them on the plates with forks. These he balanced in his hands as he made his way toward the screen door. Scruff rose, nose in the air, his front legs stretched to meet Pops's heels.

"Smell that, Wade? Hmm? Made us a pie this morning," Pops called out, bumping his hip against the door. It shushed behind him as he walked through it and onto the porch.

Pops would have been smacked for not responding to an adult when spoken to, had smacked Wade's own father. He worried he'd let Wade have it soon. Best if the boy'd stayed home. Yet, there Wade sat hunched, like a bent tree, with an invisible weight planted directly between his shoulders. His head full of curly hair dangled again over that phone.

Pops set the plate next to the boy's hip, creaking as he crouched. Wade'd taken to sitting on the edge of the porch now, not in the chair at the table with Pops like he used to before the phone.

"Scruff. Here," Pops commanded as the dog nudged the pie, then Wade's leg, his tail wagging like a flag in the wind. The dog obeyed, resting near the table. Wade didn't even look up.

Full, golden light now shone on the porch and on the boy. Pops hesitated, then rose to sit next to Wade on the porch floor, meeting

Wade where he was. Pops then stretched out the creaks, his legs dangling over the edge of the porch.

"Hey. Pie's getting cold." He smiled, nudging the boy's shoulder.

"You mind? I'm in the middle of somethin'," Wade mumbled, his eyes on the screen.

"Sorry," Pops sighed, a recognizable and simmering heat creeping up his back. He looked up at the land in front of him: stone walls broken by division, boulders out of place lying scattered among the overgrown, original two hundred acres of pasture sold off in pieces for taxes, for survival. Someone started a mower off in the distance.

"How's Jules?" Pops asked, grasping for any topic that might bond the two of them, trying to mend an invisible wall and extinguish his growing heat.

"I dunno. She's with Mom. Call Mom if ya wanna know." Pops coughed, prying his eyes from the land to Wade. Scruff made his way from the table to Pops's back, plunking himself behind his master.

Pops's ears began to ring. Was it the memory of the backhand to his own head when he'd experimented with independence a little too soon? Or was it the rising temperature of his own blood?

Rather than erupt as his own father had done, he turned away from Wade. The view north calmed him a bit. Most of the ten acres sat on this side. This was the way he remembered life, quintessential New England farmland that went on forever, it seemed, and with it, traditional values, hard work, discipline, respect, and easy conversations. Folks used to look at one another when they conversed. With modern times, discipline changed. He had to be more patient now, more controlled in what he said and did.

He wouldn't give up on himself or Wade, couldn't, really, because Wade was the future.

"Ever think of lookin' up, Wade?" Pops asked.

"Huh?" Wade responded.

"You know, at the world around you instead of only what's on that device?" Pops asked, turning to look at his grandson.

"Whatever," Wade said. Then, pausing, he gazed into Pops's narrow blue eyes and set down the phone. Those eyes of Pops were dangerous things. They reminded Wade of that too deep, very dark well on the far side of the last ten acres—the one he'd been warned about going near because no one knew how deep it was or what was inside it or if it even went on forever.

"Sorry," Wade quickly added. A silence as heavy and thick and dense as the pie sat between them.

"Look out there." Pops pointed east, toward the sun. "What do you see?" he asked Wade.

A ping from the phone stole Wade's eyes, his attention. His hand reached for it, then he stopped. Instead, his eyes followed Pops's finger.

"Nothin', really. Dad's house. A bunch of smoke from the factory. Cars." Wade shrugged, picking up his phone, but leaving it off.

Sitting taller, Pops gazed at the scene before him. Henry had sold off most of his share of the land to the factory, and yes, that had changed things. There were the creditors to pay. The rehab clinic. The divorce. The child support. All the excuses and all the mistakes.

Pops saw the way things were, the way they should have stayed, the ways they could have been before the far too many messes. Somehow there must be middle ground, that land between what was and what is. Walls could be mended, stones put back in place. He needed Wade to be the link to goodness that was lost in Henry. He needed Wade to see what he still saw in, and hoped for, the world.

"Look again," Pops said. Scruff shifted against his back and sat up, moving toward Pops's hand.

Wade sighed. He set down the phone once more. He'd grown up playing this game with Pops, but he was thirteen now, almost a man. He closed his eyes, rested them, then opened them once again.

The old oak in front of the porch glistened lime green with early leaves as the sun behind it rose higher. Various shades of green, in fact, dotted the landscape. The dirt drive that connected the two houses sent up a mist from last night's cold. A line of geese flew overhead. Wade leaned forward to look past Pops, at the view to the north, where the old well lay hidden: field, trees, forest—his endless playground.

"Jules is good. She likes her new school. Mom's gotten better too," Wade said. He picked up the pie and took a bite. Apple, his favorite.

"Dad's doin' better. He made dinner last night. Got up for work this mornin'," Wade continued. Pops always made the best pie.

Pops nodded. It took hard work and the patience of an oak to get where you wanted to go sometimes.

A flash of yellow rumbling up the road signaled the bus.

"Gotta go, Pops. Bus is here," Wade said, as he set down the plate a little too hard and grabbed his phone, the backpack sagging on his shoulders. Scruff rose and followed the boy to the edge of the stairs. But Wade forgot the dog and jogged to the bus.

Pops reached out one hand to embrace his old pet, and after setting down his own plate lifted the other hand to wave to Wade. As he slid off the porch to stand, he heard a knock. Looking up, Pops saw Wade, wide-eyed, smiling, his hand waving from inside the window as the bus drove down the road and into town.

MRS. MAGOON'S BEHIND
Carlene M Gadapee

A sure sign of spring, more reliable than crocuses

and tulips, was Mrs. Magoon's upturned behind.

Her Subaru, hatch wide open and hazards blinking,

would be snugged to the curb, and there she'd be,

floppy hat firmly on her graying head, gloved hands

in the dirt. She planted small pocket gardens, curated

and tidy, beautifying the hidden and forgotten spaces

between buildings, at stop lights, tucked into buckets

and concrete planters, a colorful pop of joy, peeking

out from rock wall borders. I wonder who takes care

of those little gardens, now that Mrs. Magoon is gone?

They aren't as pretty without her tan-culotted behind.

TIME FOR A SHOWER

John Grey

All it needs is some rain around here.
The land doesn't need to tell me that
but it does.
The weary pasture cries out,
"I can't do this on my own."
Even the toppled fence posts
would prefer to mildew and rot
from the inside
than sear like bullock skulls.
Every silence is about the weather.
Unworked fields. Mute birds.
Uninspired seeds.
A cloud float in
from the horizon,
with patches of gray
like those shadows on the moon.
But from below
it's like a drifting safe
to which no one knows the combination.
This landscape feels as if
it once held its breath in expectation,
an expectation never realized.
So it gritted and gripped
until its lungs gave out.
To cap off death's allegory,
I see, between a sorry-looking grove of trees,
an old abandoned shack,
its derelict partner of a barn.
Someone tried to make themselves a life here.

But then a drop of rain
taps on my shoulder,
And another splats gently on my head.
The weather has finally broken
but like a patron who arrives at the theater
long after the actors took their bows.
Finally, the cloud splits open
like a wet paper bag.
It rattles the roof of that shack.
I know what it's saying.
"We'll make a farmhouse of you yet."

I WISH I COULD SEE IN COLOR
Cassidy Cyr

ROCKY HERITAGE
Brenda Anderson

It was a warm spring morning in 1928. Solomon finished his coffee and headed out the door. He was eager to get into the field and start working on his stone walls. The dairy cows had been in the barn all winter. With warm days coming, they would want to get outside and stretch their stiff bones in the pasture.

Solomon knew he needed to make a barway between the fields so he could rotate his herd and still have a hayfield. As he picked up rock after rock, he thought of all the hands before his. The rocks he was touching were placed there by generations before him. His great grandfather bought the farm back in the 1800s, soon after he arrived from Sweden. Now, the farm was Solomon's. Someday he would pass it on to his son, Marcus. Thoughts of gratitude filled his head and his heart. He looked out across the fields and admired the view. If he squinted, he could see chimney smoke from the house over the hill. For this moment though, he was alone. His contemplation was only shattered by the sound of crows and the crack of stacking rough rock. This, Solomon thought, is my livelihood, my peace, and my future.

* * *

Marcus's wife got up early and drove the kids to school. As she made a U-turn in the driveway, she handed him a large drive-thru coffee, kissed him goodbye and headed off to work. This treat would make today's chores more bearable. He needed to move the barway in the west pasture. It was wide enough for his tractor, but now it needed to accommodate a large wagon too. Ten years ago, the dairy cows were replaced by vegetables. There was not enough money in milk production to support his growing family. In fact, he had to sell one of the pastures to a developer, just to pay bills. He was glad his dad, Solomon, never lived to see land sold.

If Marcus did not look south, he still saw a pristine landscape of open fields and stone walls. He could always hear the chaos though, of forty new homes and roads. He picked up rocks and thought of all his ancestors that had grown the farm. What would they think of him needing to make room for hayrides to a pumpkin patch? The stone walls used to fence in cows. Now the barriers separated crops and made a scenic backdrop for people to take autumn family pictures.

The Vietnam War recently ended, and people yearned for a simpler way of life. He lifted the rocks and thought of all the strength it took to build the walls initially. If the rocks could talk, the stories they would tell of humans, weather and changing times. Marcus was grateful for the life he had and the chance to share this beautiful place with his children.

* * *

Andy swallowed his coffee and felt the acid hit his stomach. He moved the bulldozer forward and watched the barway fall into a chasm of dirt. Out of the corner of his eye, he saw his dad, Marcus, watching him from the front porch. Even from a distance he could feel the anguish radiating from him, because he felt it too. He remembered good times on the farm, when people bought produce, fresh eggs and pumpkins.

That was before big box stores and delivery services. Now, ordering groceries online was how people shopped. He heard the crash of rock hitting rock and it sounded like the end of the world. It felt like the end, Andy thought. Now, this sacred land was being cleared for a distribution center. How ironic was that? Last night, he and his dad talked about the stone walls that were built with sweat and pride. It was decided that the corporate buyer would not have the chance to destroy the rocks. The natural farm fences, however, along with their heritage, would be buried under the rich earth.

"I am grateful for the memories," Andy said, as tears ran down his face. He got off his dozer and picked up a small, flat rock. This farm was meant to be a legacy for his children and grandchildren. Farmers were like rocks, solid and uncomplicated. But even they could be broken. Andy fell to his knees and buried the rock with his fingers. His ancestors had touched this rock with their hands. Continuing with their tradition, would be his last offering. A wall of stones built with purpose and buried with progress.

REVETMENT
Melissa Dorval

Stone by stone and boulder by boulder, we were
Built, rock wall, safeguarding contentment
The worst storms passed; from the past, we are free
Deserved and new, blissful envelopment

Devoted strength and durability
Smitten since autumn's final garnet leaf
We give each other life's tranquility
Shielding waves' energy like coral reef

Adoring laughter as the ocean sprays,
Green amethyst eyes beholden no doubt.
We hold on tight in the spindrift bouquet,
Hand in hand, it's you and I hereabout

We triumph over untamed sea
Love as if Oeagrus and Calliope

OLD FRIENDS

Karen E. Wagner

1.
Sweet reflections
meadows primed with dew.
Sight of rabbits' transparent ears
blur of hummingbirds at still-wrapped
cherry buds. A presence
over there in shadow
between the spruce and oak tree.

You point at the sway of new-yellow forsythia
by the brook since that downpour.
All while the sun appears to gobble the moon
in a voracious fit.

Moon shadows and mist
season my Sunday,
an out-of-pace hint
of a nonsensical chatbot
weaves my words and thoughts
into fibers of my finest cloth.

2.
My stars, so many countries I have traveled
yet prefer to return to simple delights
of yellow birds and new grass blades.
Compared to life drawn from the heavens
drifting down halls of Shogun's castle
among Samurai armed with swords.
Make ready for battle in the aura
of the Jaguar Throne at Uxmal where Mayan
warriors come to worship their man-made god.
Exploding in kaleidoscope colors on the Alaskan
north slope, a few natives and polar bears silhouetted
against immense painted falls.

3.
Braid middle to left then middle to right
with the occasional bead for charm.
Dressed in colors like a marigold spray.

See what I hold is a garden salad of mind
topped with cherry tomatoes and vinaigrette.

Soon we approach the old rock wall that
divides our farm from yours.
You go your way. I'll turn homeward
calling Rusty to follow me. We'll
meet again next week to see what's changed.

PICKING SQUASH AND DIGGING POTATOES

Karen E. Wagner

He brings me stuffed squash blossoms
to show me the goodness of vines full
of ripe yellow gold.
It's not quite friendship
more like mentoring.
He delights in showing me the ways
of the earth.

He indulges in the thick soil
of rotting black walnut trees
that cake his nails,
he won't dare scrub.
And paired with a grouchy wife.

I'm an across-the-road neighbor, a world apart.

We watch hawks dive bomb freshly tilled
meadow rows where robins pause to listen
for worms. In the natural order, hawks
prey on robins instead
and that worm goes free.

He teaches me
the mystery of plants.
How a carrot weeps
when it's pulled from the earth.
How broccoli bleeds
when the flowers are cut.
Sometimes we eat *of* these plants
and leave them to flourish.
Other times we consume the heart of the plants
and destroy them. Acting as though
we're innocent.
None of these plants willfully
relinquish their spirit.

The regard he shows
for chestnuts.
He cautions me not to crush
their spiny shells with my boots
for fear of marring the nuts
which he roasts to eat.
Similarly, one doesn't yank
but gently twists a pear from the tree.
I learn a tomato is ripe when I nudge it
and it rolls into my palm.

I acquire respect for nature
from this old man. Not easily taught
but felt.
I sense a meadow garden, the remainder
of his farm. If permitted, I intervene.
Chase the weeds away.
Relocate the pests. Inform the marmots
the fields are more bountiful
over that rock wall. Tell the Blue Jays
to leave those raspberries for me.

The old farmer looks on and smiles.
My work in his garden is helpful
and his old bones rebel at the bends and curls.
When he thinks of his death he mourns
the abrupt end of his harvesting.

Thank-you to the farmer, the sower and the reaper.
How else would we ever know that potatoes
cry when dug from the earth?

A FATHER'S GUIDE TO BUILDING A ROCK WALL

James Thibeault

Building a rock wall is like jazz…

Yeah, he liked the sound of that in his head. It was a great opener. Mysterious, intriguing.idn't know where it was going to lead.

Rick was thinking out his guide to rock wall building while watching his kids play in the field behind him. Occasionally, he would look over and see Todd and Charlie doing something in the distance by the swing set. As long as he could see them, and they weren't dead, it was pretty much alright. He turned back to his rock wall, grabbed another stone from the pile, and continued to ponder.

> *Building a rock wall is like jazz. While there is a set of rules, it's unpredictable what you're going to be left with. A lot of the skill is working from improvisation. There's a lot of wrong ways to blow a note, just like picking the wrong stone to place on top of another. However, the right stone and the right moment is also just as …*

Just as what? Mysterious? Tempting? No, those all sounded wrong. He opened his phone to look for some synonyms.

"Dad?"

Enigmatic … Shadowy … Peculiar …

"Dad!"

Unique! That was good.

> *However, finding the right stone and the right moment is also just as unique as finding that right sound out of a dozen possibilities.*

"Dad!"

Rick looked up from his phone, trying to locate the sound. Then, he realized it was one of his sons. A bit of panic rose up in him. He turned around to see both kids staring at him. Somehow, they had managed to be just a few steps away. Rick quickly scanned them. No blood, no missing limbs. All was good.

"What? I'm working."

"Charlie was showing me this video of XZ-Mayhem, and XZ managed to get a 3X kill while only using a bamboo attachment on his blade."

"That's nice."

"And, and after that. XZ did a jump spin with primitive shutdown! It was pretty cool."

"Okay." Rick awkwardly balanced a mid-tier rock in his hands. He looked over to Charlie who was scrolling through his phone.

"Do … you want to see the video, Dad?" asked Todd.

"Oh, um. Not right now, Toddy. How 'bout you go back to playing with Charlie?"

"We've been playing for like 20 minutes on the swings," replied Charlie, still scrolling through his phone.

"Well, when I was your age, I played outside until 9pm!"

Charlie looked up. "We can be out until 9?"

"No, of course not."

"Oh, well whatever. Come on, Todd, let's go peel more paint off the rusty swing set."

Charlie walked away as if his phone was a compass, leading him to the right destination. Todd toddled a few steps, then turned back to Rick. "You want to see some of the paint? Charlie scraped some off to make it look like a wee-wee."

"He did wha—Charlie! No making wee-wees with Todd around!"

"Can you say the actual anatomical word?"

"Don't give me sass, I'll come right over there!"

"Like you would."

"What was that?"

"Nothing."

Rick squeezed the rock until his hands were red. He glared at Todd silently until Todd awkwardly caught up with his brother. After taking a few deep breaths, Rick turned back to his wall and tried to figure where this one stone would best fit. Beside him, there were hundreds of rocks in a pile—delivered to him by a buddy with a pickup truck who had a lot of stone he wanted to get off his property. The rock he had in his hand might not be the best rock for this exact spot, but in Rick's mind it was more of using what you had and fitting it in the best spot at the moment. He stared intently at the rocks he had assembled. He listened, smelled, and absorbed the moment, until he knew where the rock needed to go. Gingerly, he lowered it down into the pile of organized chaos. After a moment, he let his fingers go, praying it wouldn't topple the rest of the rocks. Fortunately, it stayed.

Now only two thousand more stones to go, he thought. He went back to planning his rock wall guide. There was something he was just thinking about,something good. Oh, it was about the rock in his hand.

The rock that you've selected might not always be the best rock to place on the wall, but it is impossible to sift through a mountain of stones to always determine the best one. Therefore, you must accept that what you have in your hand will have a home on your wall.

Perfect. Just poetry right there. After he laid a few more rocks, he'd go in, have dinner, and then type up all the stuff he had been thinking in his head. Who knows? After he wrote all of this down, he could turn this into a book. He could sell it online and be the stone guy. Rock Wall Rick. That sounded good. Rock Wall Rick's Guide to Rock Building. Fantastic! He placed another rock on the wall, as gently as a newborn, when—

"Dad!"

Rick flinched. The rock tumbled and fell near his feet, and he dodged quickly enough so it landed on the grass instead of his toes.

"Jesus! You can't shout like that."

"Sorry, Dad."

"What the hell is it?"

"Charlie kicked me in the leg and didn't say sorry."

"Say you're sorry, Charlie."

"He's being annoying."

Rick did his fatherly speed-walk up to Charlie. The boys were a distance away, so there was plenty of time to build up terror in the boys. By the time Rick reached them, the two were stiff and silent.

"Charlie. Say sorry."

"Sorry."

"Good. Todd. Don't be annoying."

"But—"

"No. Stop it. Play on the swing. No peeling the paint. Just enjoy this wonderful swing set that I bought for you with my money. Hell, it's five years old and you never touch it."

"It's rusty, Dad," said Charlie. "Look at the chain."

Rick observed the chain at the top and gave it a few lazy wiggles.

"It's fine. Now, I don't want a peep out of you two until I finish the last yard."

"But, we're bored," moaned Charlie.

"Then don't be."

"Can you hang out with us?" asked Todd. "Charlie likes to pretend he's an astronaut going into space. I'm the ground guy."

"Ground control, dummy."

"Dad, he called me—"

"What did I say about being annoying?"

"Sorry."

"Enjoy being astronauts. Remember, there's no air in space, so that means you can't scream."

"But—" pleaded Todd.

"Almost done." Rick walked back to his unfinished wall. He heard the squeaks of the swing set but did not bother to look back and see what they were doing. He had such great thoughts in his head, and he wanted to make sure that he didn't lose momentum. Rick needed to hold firm his thoughts, make sure they would last for a while. Suddenly, a wave of inspiration made him grin. Despite Todd's shouts behind him, he meditated on his ideas while laying more rocks.

This is your legacy. Unlike wood, plastic, or even concrete, a stone wall will stay a stone wall for a very long time. In New England, you'll walk through woods and see odd stone walls appear next to trails. What are these borders? They used to be boundary markers for farms. However, the farms disappeared, and the trees grew back. Time moved on, but the stones remained. That is what you are building when you construct a rock wall. You are building a lasting legacy that will be observed and remembered long after you die. Think of how your children will remember—

"I CAN'T STOP IT!"

Rick turned around to see Charlie uncontrollably flying on the swing set, screaming. He swayed back and forth like an aggressive metronome as Todd shuffled with his hands and feet, unsure how to help. Rick dropped his rock and ran to the children.

"Don't panic, just relax," shouted Rick.

"I can't stop, I can't stop. The whole set is shaking."

Rick looked at the metal frame, it was beginning to lift itself off the ground. He thought he secured—it didn't matter.

"Dad," cried Todd. "Help him."

"I will. Your Dad's got this." With a deep breath, he gently walked up to Charlie,his face nauseously white. "Charlie, I'm going to stop you, just don't kick me."

"It's rocking!"

While Charlie was on the upswing, Rick stood directly in his path. Dad would be a barrier, unmoving. Charlie tucked in his legs when he swung towards his father, but Rick still received two knees to the chest. It pushed Rick back, but he never fell backwards. The fatherly wall held.

"Thank you, thank you!" Charlie hugged his Dad tight. Todd, feeling left out, hugged Rick by the ankles.

"What were you doing?"

"Being astronauts."

"Well, you flew too close to the sun."

"Sorry, Dad."

"I'm sorry, I should have been keeping a better eye on you two. Let's take a break from the swings, what do you two want to do?"

"How's the wall coming?" asked Charlie, peering over Rick's shoulder.

"Um, good."

"Can we build it?" shouted Todd. He was jumping and squirming in excitement.

"Can we?" Charlie smiled at his Dad.

"Uh, sure. But let's talk about—"

Before he had a chance to explain, the two boys ran to the stone wall and haphazardly placed rocks where they shouldn't have been. It was beginning to look like rubble instead of a delicate monument. Rick was about to shout when he thought about his guide.

Think of how your children will remember.

Rick went over to his sons and showed him where to place the big heavy one that they were both trying to lift. Together, they would build a very mediocre stone wall. It wouldn't be one for the ages.

A PASTURE OF MORROW
Jayden Lindsay

A pasture of sorrow
A pasture of morrow
I walk towards it
Dreaming
Wishing
Hoping
I want the life I can not have
Why can't I?
It is there for the taking so I need to take the leap
It is right there
Just across the pasture of morrow
If I can just cross it I'll be free
But, something
holds me back
I look back at it
It is everything, wanting me to stay back.
I do not listen to it
I take the leap
Run across the field
As I reach the other side I see
That something is there, but it is better. It is filled
with love
With hope
With friendship
Always cross that open pasture
The grass is greener on the other side

THE WALL
Jayden Lindsay

A wide open wall

One that will forever stay

Stood high above others

GAP

Karen Durlach

Spine-breaking muscle-challenging stone
on New England stone
stops

restarts
after the granite gap
where deer tracks imprint the snow
travel through, scrape down
to leafy beds nearby

Mouse evidence skitters
back and forth across the empty space,
perpendicular to the passersby

A basic boundary,
our yard, theirs,
once-fields now tall in regrowth

Offerings left
on the altar of the gap,
rejected cat kibble,
well-stewed bones,
snap-trapped house invaders,
unexpected morsels
atop this well-traveled stony way

Game camera catches the thankful—
coon, coyote, possum,
someone else's cat,
even an owl,
choking down a frozen carcass.

THE RAPTOR
Ed Ahern

For as long as he could remember, Jamie talked to birds. Well, not exactly. Blue Jays and sparrows, mourning doves and crows all flew down around him, so close he could touch them if he wanted to. Even sparrow hawks, which never tried to eat the sparrows while they were near Jamie. The birds made soft sounds, not loud squawks or caws, more like they were clearing their throats.

When he went out for recess in kindergarten, the other children watched him closely, for soon the birds would land next to Jamie, and cluster to stay close to him. As they squirreled and chirped Jamie would nod, pucker his lips and chirp back at them.His teachers and the guidance counselor quickly noticed this peculiar situation and called his parents.

"Not to worry," said his dad. "It's been that way from the first day we took him outside in a baby carriage. I think he gives off some kind of odor which attracts the birds."

Other children took videos. They would show them to their parents, who posted pictures on social media. This led to stories being written about Jamie, now known as the 'Bird Boy.'

His parents took him to doctors and counselors to find out what was wrong with him. His mother and father wanted to stop the behavior, for, Jamie's mental health aside, the birds left droppings behind them. But no one could help. Jamie's mom and dad loved him very much and decided they could put up with the birds for his sake.

Jamie was asked many times if he could understand what the birds were saying, and he would half smiled and nod. But in fact, it was much more than that. He and the birds shared sensations. Jamie knew the taste of a beetle, the rustling of a chick inside its shell, the itch of feather infesting mites.

His parents insisted that Jamie open up to the birds only when he was alone with no one watching, and he almost always obeyed. Once there were no more public shows, the media moved on to the next sensation and Jamie was forgotten. But not by the birds. There were always little groups of starlings, geckos and cardinals near his house or school, waiting for Jamie to become receptive to them.

One day, when he was seventeen, and in the backyard alone, a shiny black bird landed next to him. It was twice the size of a crow, with a thicker beak. The raven hopped onto Jamie's shoulder and leaned in, making harsh noises. Jamie's smile disappeared as he listened closely. He shook his head no twice, but the raven kept rasping into his ear.Finally, with a worried expression, Jamie nodded yes. He walked back into their house.

"Mom," he said, "I need to borrow the car for a couple hours."

"What for, Jamie?"

He didn't want to lie, but he told her something not entirely true. "Just a favor for a friend. I need to pick something up for him."

"That's fine, dear. You know where the keys are."

Jamie unlocked the car and opened up the passenger side door so the raven could hop in, for its wingspan was much too wide to fly into the car.

"Which way?" Jamie asked.

A raven's voice sounds like steel nails scratching glass, but Jamie didn't mind. He had to detour twice because a raven has no need for roads and only knew the way by flying straight.Jamie was relieved when they finally came to the end of a rough trail, for he wasn't sure his mother's car could handle the potholes much longer. They were in deep woods, facing a steep, high embankment.The raven hopped out of the car and gave Jamie his last directions, warning him of the dangers ahead.

"It is a raptor with a silken tongue. It will tell you to go away before you die, or to spare its life as an act of kindness, or to take a few of the gold coins and go away. Do none of these things, for it is a prince of liars who is hungry. Instead, offer to help it die well."

"I don't want to kill anything."

"I did not say kill. If you can help my friend, you may take what you find. Listen…"

As Jamie listened, he nodded his head. "I can do that," he said.

He climbed up the steep embankment, almost a cliff, until he reached a shallow cave. Before entering the cave, he looked down in awe at the rock walls and open meadows below. When he entered the cave, he noticed a reek of dead things, and Jamie saw scattered bones of birds, cats and small dogs. He urgently wanted to turn back, but he'd given his word, and entered the cave.There, sprawled on the dirt floor was the biggest bird he'd ever seen. "You're, you're a condor aren't you?"

The condor's voice sounded like the breaking of rotten wood. "My followers bring me meat and jays and crows bring me shiny things. If you have brought me something worthwhile, I might spare you."

Even in the dim light, Jamie could see the condor's ragged feathers and gaunt body. He suspected that if the condor could move at all it would be haltingly.

"I bring you release."

"Then you must die to feed me."

Jamie felt his fear tingle in his hands, but said. "You could not fly, or even hop well for many years. But I will set you free."

The bird spread its wings so wide that they touched the sides of the cave. "I am Vultur Gryphus, the largest of my kind, and you are prey. Who are you to tell me anything?"

Jamie stepped back in fear, but continued to talk. Eventually, Vultur Gryphus bobbed its head up and down. Jamie stepped forward and the condor folded its wings tightly against its body. He placed the bird under his arm and clasped his two hands together. As light as it was, it was too large to hold with one arm. Jamie carefully picked his way out of the cave. Thirty yards from the edge of the cliff he ran toward it. Just before he got to the drop off, he threw the condor up and out over the edge.

As the bird spread its ragged wings it dropped Then caught in an updraft the condor could spread its wings. It flew high about the open meadows, and it vanished into the sky in seconds.

Jamie, panting, whispered, "Fly now for as long as you can, and fall magnificently." He walked back into the cave, then slowly and carefully climbed back down the embankment. The raven was waiting.

"You gave my master the help I couldn't."

"Yes, and I think he was grateful. Do you want a ride back?"

"Don't be absurd."

"Please, if you can, return and tell me more."

"As I can I shall."

Ravens are clumsy launchers, and Jamie watched it awkwardly hop onto a low branch, flap its wings and take off. He walked back to his mom's car. His pockets were bulging and clinking. He needed to figure out a story to explain all the gold coins and rings.

WEDNESDAY NIGHT RESPITE

Thom Brucie

On Wednesday evening
Natalie leaned her head against
The pocket of the kitchen wall
Hunting a strange sound,
Like an Aeolian whisper
Through plumes of sweet grass.

The music of yearning
Toggled ancient dreams
To fresh desires
Of pine and sycamore,
'Till the half-moon rose
Above the kitchen walls
To empty them
Of monotony
And stainless steel pots.

Away she let her heart-dreams glide,
To lull her labored day to rest,
And thinking she finally found a forest for her joy,
She canned the memory
Like a jam.

A TRUE STORY – AGNIG ADVICE
Barbara Vosburgh

A heron showed up in my side yard, which was unusual since the only water was a trap somewhere on the golf course beyond the trees in the backyard. At first, I was so excited and started taking pictures.

The second day was not so happy for me. He grabbed one of my chipmunks that I feed every day. How dare he! There is a rock wall between my house and my neighbor. Of course he took the chipmunk I had named Long Tail to the neighbor's yard. Long Tail was hanging in the heron's mouth by the head trying to escape, so of course I had to try to save him.

I tried climbing the wall. It wasn't too high, and I could do it the year before. I lost my footing. Fell backwards. Phone and glasses went flying. Lay there yelling, "Help. Please help!" my neighbor eventually came out. He thought it was a bird yelling at first until he heard the word "please."

I asked him to get my phone and glasses so I could call my daughter who was in the house. They helped me up and I stumbled toward the door. My daughter had to go get my grandson after school. I was alone trying to sit, lay down, or walk. Unsuccessful.

When my daughter came home, I was passing out off and on. She called the ambulance, and off I went to the ER. They found a place on my back that was broken and a broken rib. They also found internal bleeding. I'm on blood thinners, so that was no surprise. Med-flight was called.

It was my first, and hopefully last, helicopter ride. Trying to keep a positive attitude, I asked if I could fly it myself. I couldn't even move. The crew was wonderful on the ten minute ride to the Trauma Center in Worcester.

It took a full year to completely recover from the injuries. A long year, but I found ways of doing things I wasn't supposed to do.

The moral of this story is don't climb a rock wall without help. Above all, don't fall in your seventies. Finally, let nature be nature. Difficult lessons to learn. A year and some months later, I am still afraid of falling, but keep on going. Follow me for more aging advice...LOL

RUMINATIONS

Barbara A Reynolds

You think I don't remember
the day the cows crept across the rotted fence
fleeing their hillside pasture like prisoners refused parole.
They scrambled down the rock-studded slope
winding their curious way between brambles and boles.
Their hooves clipped the crowds of skunk cabbage leaves
releasing a gassy cadaverous scent that marked the brazen descent
on the small-footed path to our street.
They lingered on lawns carelessly chewing their cud, while you,
afraid those soft-snouted raiders would launch an attack
(as if I could become a herbivore's savory snack)
made me stow my trike and get indoors
until the leather-bearing herd was moored.
But you were never mindful of the many days
I wound my curious way
around the trees and past the brambles,
skirting the stinky skunky leaves,
tripping up the rocky hillside path alone
then crawling through the broken slatted fence to roam.

THE BURDEN OF STONES
Michelle Elliott

When spring came to the farm, it meant one thing to Richard Wilson and his only brother Sam: stone season. Not that Richard minded. The season signaled that the little Enfield school house a mile downriver stayed closed for a spell. All hands, large and small, made ready the fields left fallow the year before, neighbor helping neighbor.

Father spent the dreary winter in the barn preparing for spring, scraping the plow blades of rust and dried mud. Richard escaped the gaggle of siblings corralled in the farmhouse, perched high on a barn's thick beam, wincing at the sharp rake of metal as Father worked the heavy file.

With school postponed, the barren field lay before them like a tangled knot waiting to be untied. Women and young children uprooted and tore away weeds, heaping them on the burn piles, while men and boys pried and plucked fieldstones from the earth. The cold bite of winter still clung to the muddy ground, and the rough stones made soft skin dry and cracked.

In the circle around the burn pile at midday, the workers shared bread, dried fruit, and cider. Richard slipped Sam a few apple pieces, hoping to bring some cheer to his grimaced face.

"Why are there so many?" Sam said. He held his small, calloused palms up to the fire's warmth.

"What? Fieldstones?" Richard answered, loosening the laces from the oversized work shoe crafted special for his clubbed foot.

Sam nodded. "Didn't we clear this pasture last year?"

"Not this one. Dirt spits them stones back to the top over time like a potato crop."

Sam pondered Richard's words. "Well, it ain't right. Once they're gone, they should stay gone."

A few years older than Sam, Richard was used to his brother's protests when it came to chores. His little brother had yet to see the value in tending the fields that fed them.

Sam scowled and pulled his thick wool cap tighter over his ears.

When the group returned to the field, Sam remained planted in his spot, his clear blue eyes fixed on the fire's bright flame.

Richard gave him a brotherly shove. "C'mon."

"No," Sam said and crossed his arms over his chest. "I'm not picking rocks no more." His whiny voice held the timbre of a stubborn eleven-year-old boy.

Richard took a long, steady breath, then slowly released it. Father wasn't keen on shirking a duty and even less keen on disobedience. The switch that hung in the woodshed ensured that neither was commonplace in the Wilson house.

"Then I reckon you won't play a little game I had in mind," Richard said, turning to go.

"What game?"

Richard paused. "Let's say them stones ain't no stones, but potatoes and the first one to clear and stack ten barrows on them walls wins."

"Wins what?"

"Loser mucks the stalls for a week."

That was all Sam needed, a silly game to disguise work as play. The rest of the day they whooped and hollered, laying the stones on the long walls that outlined the fields and the smaller one that held the family cemetery. Richard moved half a pace slower, intentionally losing to his brother.

The following week, Richard grinned, shoveling the manure from the cow stalls, paying no mind to the extra work knowing he'd saved Sam from the switch.

A few years later, southern cannons sounded a different spring, one of fighting and battles between North and South. Held back by his foot, twisted and bent, not meant for marching, Richard watched as Sam, with shoulders broad like Father's, marched to war instead.

The Wilson family gathered at the Enfield common and bid him farewell when he stepped off to join the blue-uniformed wave of sons and brothers, fathers and uncles, farmers mostly, to fight for Lincoln's cause. Sam never swayed nor staggered under the heavy pack, as his feet fell into step with the drum boy's hollow beat. Mother held her swell of tears until the rag-tag Massachusetts regiment disappeared.

Sam sent word now and then. The scrawled writing told of foul weather, rancid bacon, and battles won and lost, always ending with a fond remembrance of home.

"Tell Richard to mind them field potatoes," he'd write. *"He'll know what I'm sayin'."*

After a time, the stream of letters ran dry. Mother took turn after turn on the front porch. Her unflinching eyes searched deep into the distant pastures, waiting for word, or the figure of her son coming home. But he did not. She passed, never knowing his fate, or reading the telegraph post of him gone missing, her spirit forever walking the porch.

The family often visited Sam's stone, etched only with his birthdate. Richard couldn't bring himself to join them. The respect paid, and the prayers offered felt wasted on an empty grave. Instead, Richard took solace walking the fields of youthful, leafy corn, acres of viridescent shafts, only waist high, yet straight and promising.

Evenings when the sun slipped behind the western hills, Richard and his father sat on the porch and viewed the same pastoral scene as Mother did when she walked from porch end to porch end.

Gone four years with the bloody war finally over, Sam's absence was a haunting, a place of neither life nor death, and on that porch one evening Richard told his father of his decision to leave.

"Crops are comin' along fine." Richard said, passing the shine bottle back to his father, careful to avoid the man's mournful eyes. "I'll be back by mid fall—early enough to husk out the corn."

"Come back when you come back," his father said, unable to speak Sam's name. He took a long pull from the bottle and set it down hard on the wooden crate between them, settling the matter.

The following day Richard cinched a supply sack to the mule Father insisted he take. There was no send-off like Sam's. No drum boy to keep time or waving town folk. No scuff of boots or flag bearing sentry, just Father and Richard's three wide-eyed sisters, all too young yet for marrying.

Father nodded and headed back to the house. The girls stayed a few moments longer before they, too, turned away.

The road, no more than a meandering cow path, stretched before him. Resolute and eager for an answer, Richard gave the old mule a kick and the journey to Sam began.

TRUTH

Kathy Bennett

Be not afraid,
frayed by anxiety to your weary heart
that dwells in stone-cold crevices
within dark and shapeless shadows.
Be not afraid.
Come into the light
of the sun of justice,
and rest like a liberated lizard
atop the rock of his Redeemer.
Be not afraid
to let go of the scales
that block your eyes,
Your mind,
Your memory…
Honest to goodness truth
Shall make you *free*.
Be not afraid.

TWO SIDES OF A ROCK WALL
Diane Kane

Senator John Bailey's secret was the furthest thing from his mind on a warm spring afternoon in Washington, DC. Bailey hailed from a New England farming town where rolling pastures seemed to go on forever, and the only walls were made of rock, many marking long-forgotten property boundaries. Although the marble walls of Washington, DC, were a stark contrast, Bailey embraced them.

"Senator Bailey, where are we going?" William, his legislative assistant, asked as he struggled to keep pace with the statesman's stride through the echoing halls of the Capitol Building.

"Outside, William, to inhale the sweet aroma of the cherry blossoms," Senator Bailey said over his shoulder as his Martino leather dress shoes clicked on the well-polished floors. "I need to clear my head of this infernal den of deceit." Bailey turned and straightened his silk tie in the reflection of William's starry-eyed admiration.

Bailey cut left into the entrance hall and exited through the tall double doors with his assistant chasing after his illustrious coattails. Descending the broad marble stairs, he shielded his eyes to adjust to the daylight. Disoriented by loud shouts and clicking cameras, he squinted into the crowd, making brief eye contact with a pretty young girl. A swarm of reporters, with video camera operators and microphones in tow, parted to let the girl step forward.

The senator's eyes lingered on her bulging belly as she jabbed her finger into the air toward him and screamed, "He's the one. Senator John Bailey, he's the father of my child!"

If Senator Bailey had actually possessed male genitals, they would have shriveled at the accusation. Instead, the nipples his once female breasts hardened in denial. John Bailey had spent almost a lifetime living a lie.

As a toddler, his parents coerced their child with pink dresses and dolls, before giving up and accepting the obvious. Bailey's father, a well connected lawyer, helped to make the necessary legal changes to transform Joan into John for all intents and purposes. Not long after, John's lawyer father divorced his wife for another woman, a trophy wife, his father liked to joke. John led a sheltered life with his mother, away from the spotlight, all the while longing to follow in the footsteps of his strong and powerful father. His mother homeschooled him, and by the time John entered college, he had buried his female identity forever, or so he thought.

A reporter pushed past the Capitol police, jolting the senator from his childhood memories. "Senator, what do you say to these accusations?" he asked, sticking a microphone in Bailey's face. "Senator, Senator!"

Bailey wiped the sweat from his brow. He did know the pregnant girl on the steps pointing her finger and claiming he fathered her child. He had befriended her in his last reelection campaign. Not even old enough to vote, she had worked tirelessly stuffing envelopes with campaign promises. Bailey was well aware at the time that she had an adolescent crush on him, or rather on the pretense of Senator John Bailey.

He had felt sorry for the forlorn girl, who lived in the projects in an unsavory part of the city. She never knew the feeling of freedom that Bailey had experienced in his youth, the open pastures and blue skies. This young girl had only ever known concrete walls that kept her contained and limited her possibilities. When they worked late at the campaign office, Bailey had driven her home in his BMW convertible. He went the long way around to give her more time to feel the exhilaration of the wind through her hair. Bailey hoped she would make good choices and break the boundaries of her lot in life.

I was only trying to protect her. I never tried to encourage her feelings, he thought.

"Senator Bailey, we need to get you inside," William shouted over the chaos.

Bailey's eyes blinked as a ticker tape of thoughts streamed through his head.

All I have to say is that I'm really a woman and couldn't possibly have gotten this young girl pregnant.

It sounded so easy, but Bailey knew nothing was simple in politics. His mind raced with thoughts of his rise to power. One of his goals in running for office had been to spearhead changes in the laws and prejudices against people like himself. He had studied political law at Harvard before he ran for Massachusetts State Representative in his late twenties, then a congressman, before he went on to win his first bid for the U.S. Senate, serving three consecutive terms. Senator John Bailey achieved his dream of emulating his father in wealth and power—with one big difference. Senator Bailey combined his prestige with the honor that his father's character so sorely lacked. Bailey championed the LGBTQ community. He filibustered for the rights of same-sex couples. Senator John Bailey became their "man" in Congress.

How brutally ironic. I've lied to everyone, including myself.

The senator self-consciously brushed the front of his double-breasted Italian suit.

William steered Bailey back up the Capitol steps, away from the rush of reporters. The senator stumbled and fell on the cold stone, attempting to escape the bloodthirsty horde. Bailey glimpsed some of his fellow congressmen and women gawking at the scene. A weak laugh escaped his lips as he realized that not one of them would step forward to defend him. Whether they believed the adolescent girl or not, they knew as well as Bailey that it's not always the truth of the accusation that kills a career; sometimes, it's only the uncertainty of the idea.

Why should they risk their careers to defend me? Bailey's stomach churned.

Two police officers broke through the crowd and picked Bailey up under the arms, whisking him through the massive double doors. Leaving him in the empty Rotunda chamber, they hurried back outside to help contain the growing unrest.

William sat beside the senator on the bench under the large mural depicting the baptism of Pocahontas. Bailey smiled at the image of the Indian princess lying on a dais, her head bowed and her hands clasped before her, as the assembled audience looked on with an array of emotions from power to pity.

"Senator, no one is going to believe that girl," William said. "Everyone knows your reputation."

Bailey looked into William's innocent eyes but couldn't find any words.

Would William think as highly of me if he knew that the real reason I always use the stalls in the men's room is that I don't have the equipment to use the urinals?

Bailey blinked back tears and began to weigh his options. Demanding a DNA test would only have confirmed his female identity.

Can I save my career by taking responsibility for the girl's child? He silently wondered.

Bailey reflected on some of his colleagues who had faced similar accusations and survived the aftermath. Still, he had seen other lengthy careers crash and burn in a media frenzy. It was all up to the whim of the news mill and the chance of a more prominent headline drawing the spotlight away from his sordid story.

William returned from talking with security. "The police have contained the crowd. I think we can leave soon," William said.

Bailey turned away to avoid William's eyes.

Is it safer to tell the public that I've misled them all along into believing that I'm a man?

Bailey could admit his deception and beg for the mercy of the voters. The LGBTQ community might forgive him, knowing what he had achieved for them in the guise of a male. He didn't doubt that male voters would seek revenge in the ballot box if he told the truth.

"Senator." A guard approached. "We will have a car for you in a few minutes so you can leave."

Bailey pressed his hands to his face. He felt the walls closing in on him.

I can run, but where can I hide? The press will already be outside my condo.

Bailey reflected on his choices. He thought about the poor pregnant girl with pity.

She has to be destitute to bring herself to this public forum.

Even so, he knew that taking responsibility for her child could ultimately prove to be the destruction of his career. If Bailey revealed he was a woman, he would be admitting to deceiving the whole country.

Either way, I very well could be speaking my last words as an elected official.

"Come on, Senator," William prodded him. "Let's go."

The choice I make today will change my life, as I know it, forever. Bailey breathed a sigh of resolve. *There is only one decision I can live with.*

The guards stood at attention as the senator squared his shoulders and walked across the hallway. They opened the entrance doors to the frenzied media. The crowd turned from the pregnant young girl and strained against the police line.

"You don't have to go out there, Senator," William pleaded.

Bailey turned and grasped the boy's shoulder. "William, there's a child about to enter this world who needs the full support of a father." Bailey looked into his eyes. "I have to stand up and be that man."

Bailey faced the crowd with his usual political prowess while his feminine feet struggled to fill his no longer familiar shoes. He imagined himself poised on a rock wall with an endless field of green, green grass beckoning him. The warm spring breeze touched his cheeks, and the smell of new beginnings filled the air.

Sometimes, truth is like a rock wall. You have to know what side of it will set you free.

"Ladies and Gentlemen." John Bailey, the male senator of Massachusetts, looked straight into the cameras and spoke clearly. "I'm going to be sincere with you today, just as I have been for my past eighteen years in the Senate."

THE WITCH AND THE WARTS
William Belisle

When I was eight years old, three small warts on my hand changed my life in ways I could never have imagined. Two sat on the side of my right index finger, rough and raised, and the third nestled near my knuckle, almost as if it had every intention of staying.

My mother, my brother, and my two sisters all lived together in a narrow house on a quiet street in Ludlow, Massachusetts, a small industrial town. My father had passed away two years earlier, leaving my mother to piece together our lives on the earnings she made as a dressmaker. Her work was exceptional—elegant gowns and wedding dresses that looked out of place in our simple home. Yet, it was hard to find enough work to keep us fed, and a few times, we went to bed hungry.

Just down the street, in a house that always seemed darker than its neighbors, lived a witch. Yes, a witch. How do I know? Because, to my eight-year-old eyes, she looked exactly like a witch should look—dressed head-to-toe in black, with shoes that clicked on the pavement, a long black dress, a shawl, and an odd, shiny black hat. She was short and wiry, with tight curls and an ominous cane that scraped on the pavement as she limped along. Her eyes were sharp and narrow, and though I rarely saw them, I imagined they could see right through me.

My mother, however, seemed unbothered by the witch. The two of them would acknowledge each other with tight-lipped nods as we walked down our street from church. They occasionally even stopped to talk. I'd heard that the witch attended Mass every day, which struck me as odd; did all witches go to church?

My mother noticed that my warts bothered me and that I kept my hands in my pockets to hide them. She told me that the witch possessed powers from beyond the grave, and urged me to pay her a visit because she could cure my warts. The idea terrified me—not because I doubted the witch's ability but because, well, she was a witch and I wanted nothing to do with her. I was certain she'd demand something terrible in return, something that I could never repay.

When my mother warned me that my warts might spread all over my body if left unchecked, my fear of the witch was replaced by a deeper dread, and I knew I had to see the witch sooner or later.

It was a chilly Sunday morning, just after church, when my mother decided it was high time to put my trepidation behind me and visit the witch for a cure. With a not-so-gentle push from my mother out the door, I had no choice but to trudge reluctantly down our street to her door. She opened it without a word, sizing me up with a knowing look before leading me silently inside. Without a question or a greeting, she gestured for me to kneel before her large, creaky rocking chair.

"Show me your hand," she said, her voice deep and gravelly. I hadn't mentioned my warts, or even said a single word to her, but I assumed the witch knew why I was there and didn't need me to tell her why I had come.

I held out my hand, and she grasped it with surprising firmness. She clicked her tongue and made the sign of the cross over each wart, mumbling words in a language I couldn't identify, a murmur that sent shivers down my spine. She pulled a penny from her purse and placed it over each wart in turn, pressing it down tightly for a few moments, as if transferring something from the coin to my skin or perhaps from my skin to the coin. After what seemed like an eternity, she closed her ritual with a solemn "Amen" and released my hand, nodding toward the door.

I was out of her house in seconds, my heart pounding, and I didn't stop running until I was safe at home. But over the next few weeks, something remarkable happened: the warts began to shrink, and soon, they were gone completely. I didn't know how or why, but the witch's power was undeniable.

Years passed, and the world changed. When Pearl Harbor was attacked, I enlisted in the army and was sent to Fort Devens for training before being deployed to England in 1943 to work with munitions.

One day, in the crowded barracks, I noticed that the adjutant—our unit's personnel officer—had hands fairly covered in warts. I couldn't help but remember the witch and what she'd done for me. Emboldened, I approached him, offering to cure his warts.

I'll admit that I had an ulterior motive: the adjutant was the keeper of the much-sought-after weekend passes.

He laughed at me and said I was crazy, loudly enough for everyone to hear. Later though, in private, he asked "Were you serious before? Do you really think you can cure them?" He was skeptical yet intrigued. "I've already tried every salve and gimmick I could find, but nothing works," he lamented. Boldly, I assured him that I could help him and after a few moments, he relented, letting me try.

Later that evening, in a darkened room, I went through the same ritual I remembered from all those years before, mimicking the witch's gestures and muttering an incantation that sounded deep and prayerful, but was little more than mumbled nonsense. I pressed a penny hard over each wart, finishing with "Amen" as if finalizing some ancient spell.

Weeks later, imagine my surprise when his warts began to slowly shrink, then vanish one by one. With a look of astonishment and gratitude, he promised me liberty passes whenever I wanted one. No one was more surprised than I was by the miraculous cure, but I was cocky enough to act as though I had done it a thousand times before.

In time, word got around and I became something of a "wart healer" among the men in my unit. They'd approach me, somewhat embarrassed, their hands outstretched, hopeful that the penny's magic might be real. It didn't work every time, but enough for me to maintain an aura of mystery. Each time I went through the motions, I tried not to chuckle at the astounding absurdity of it all. But again and again, their warts disappeared, as if their belief in my power alone had cured them.

After the war, in medical school, I learned of many more conventional treatments and techniques, but case after case revealed to me the power of the mind and the ability of the body to heal itself.

Looking back, I've thought many times how such a simple thing as my mother pushing me out the door had changed my life, how the "witch" had set me on this trajectory. I've wished many times that I could go back and thank her.

Years later, I found myself back in Ludlow, sitting in my car just down the street from where the witch's house had once stood. I looked down at my own hands—weathered, scarred, but clean of warts—and wondered if she'd ever doubted her own power, or if she'd known all along that belief was the true magic.

Had she passed her secret to me that day? Or had she merely shown me that people find faith in the most unexpected places—in pennies, in gestures, in a few muttered words?

As the sun set over Ludlow, I decided it didn't really matter, and that I would have to live with the mystery of the witch and the warts. Perhaps this was the payback the witch demanded.

FIELD OF SCHEMES

Steven Michaels

That we should tarry in the field
and daydream on end
would be a most satisfying activity.

How often do we get the chance
to watch the clouds swim in blue
while we float upon the grass bed?

Yet you seem preoccupied:
your fervent mind does not let
you simply watch the world go by.

Instead your eyes disclose their scheming:
darting around the landscape,
seeing only your mind's eye.

Come out from your mad psyche,
join me on the grass,
laugh with me at the clown-shaped cumulus.

Take a moment, maybe more;
each day a sun sets somewhere
while the puffs of white wither away.

Drifting briefly on the earth,
knowing we cannot stay;
so caught up in the planning of things.

Realizing we want
nothing more
than we already have:

save time
to rest
in peace.

HOW TO RETIRE
Mary Anne Kalonas Slack

The day Phil Baker left his manufacturing job at Bentley Tool Company, he told his buddies to be sure to drive by his house on Monday morning on their way to work. They'd been giving him a hard time with how bored and broke he'd be if he retired, so Phil wanted to make them laugh. Those who drove by saw him sitting in a recliner on his front lawn, wearing shorts and a t-shirt that said, "Officially Retired—Not my Problem Anymore," holding a giant cup of coffee in his hand. He'd erected a great big sign that read: I'm Retired and You're Not! Have a Great Day at Work!! His friends, and lots of other people going by, laughed, honked their horns, and gave him a thumbs up.

By nine-thirty, traffic had slowed, and he went back in the house. His wife Sharon was just heading out.

"Where are you off to?" Phil asked her. Sharon was a couple of years older than he was, and she'd retired over a year ago.

"To my volunteer job at the food pantry. I work on the books there every Monday morning. Want to come along?"

"No, thanks. I've got a big day planned. Golf at eleven, lunch with Roy, then I'm going fishing for a couple of hours at the pond. I'll see you at dinnertime."

Sharon was stirring a pot of pasta when Phil got home.

"Have a good day?" she asked.

"Great. Very nice. How about you?"

"I was at the food pantry all morning and I came home for lunch, talked to my sister on the phone, cleaned the bathrooms and read for awhile."

"You were busy. I'm not sure I want to be busy in my retirement. But then again, I don't want to golf every day, or fish every day. I need to find things to do. Maybe I'll clean up the yard tomorrow."

"That'd be great. I'll help. But I'm going to my book discussion group at the library at nine and then I'll stay to shelve books for a while. I'll be back by lunchtime."

Phil ate his dinner silently for a while before commenting that he didn't realize she had so many activities filling her week.

"I've found it takes time to figure out how to retire. Some people fill it with lots of activities and then weed some of them out over time. Others think that not working is the only important thing and they sit on their duffs and watch tv. Other people travel the world, but that takes a lot of money, not to mention physical stamina. I'm still figuring it out. I'm sure you will, too. This is only the first day of your retirement. Give yourself a break. Do what you feel like doing and it will all fall into place. You'll find your rhythm after a while."

Phil had to laugh at himself, worrying about this on day one. Sharon was right. He should just enjoy himself for now.

The next morning, he was sitting in his recliner enjoying a second cup of coffee and watching the morning news shows when Sharon came in to say goodbye. "I'll pick up some sandwiches for lunch and we can work in the yard later."

Phil waved goodbye and thought about what he wanted to do with the morning. Just sitting here was pretty nice. He thought about his uncle Charlie who was eighty-five and lived in an assisted living community. Phil hadn't seen him in months, so he picked up the phone and asked if he could come over to visit. Uncle Charlie said he was just on his way out to play pickleball and was planning to take a walk after that, have lunch, take a nap, and then go to a painting class in the afternoon. He had time to see him between four and five if he could make it then.

"Wow. You're awfully busy for a retired guy, Uncle Charlie," Phil observed.

"Gotta keep busy, kid. The guys who sit in their recliners and watch tv all day are dead before their time. The world is your oyster, now. A big, open field filled with possibilities. What do you plan to do today?"

Phil decided not to tell him that he was sitting in a recliner watching tv.

That afternoon, and for the next three days, Phil worked in the yard. He cleaned out flower beds, trimmed trees and shrubs, and reinforced a rock wall. He repaired the bird feeder, organized the garage, cleaned his and Sharon's cars inside and out and then waxed them until they gleamed. By Friday afternoon he was in his recliner with an ice pack on his right shoulder and a heating pad on his lower back.

"Do you think maybe you overdid a little?" Sharon said as she brought him some ibuprofen and a tall glass of water. "You have the rest of your life, you know. Do a little bit each day. You've got the time now."

Phil nodded and closed his eyes. He'd never been outstanding at anything, really. He was just a regular guy who supported his family, attended church on Sunday, went to his kids' Little League games, socialized with his neighbors. He never won any awards, but he'd never really failed at anything. Was it possible to fail at retirement?

His own father had died at seventy-two. If he was like him, that meant he had seven years to live. The thought scared him. His mother lived until eighty-five, active until the end. Maybe he'd take after her, but that was still only twenty years away. Twenty years was nothing. He needed to get off his butt and live, but doing what?

A month went by and still Phil couldn't find a rhythm to his days that felt comfortable. He did tasks around the house, played golf once a week, and went fishing on nice days. He tried playing pickleball with his uncle, but he couldn't get the hang of it. He'd been good at making tools on a machine. He was competent and confident at that job, feeling the rhythm of the machine connecting to the rhythm of his movements. He needed to find something that gave him that same satisfaction.

One Monday morning he'd decided to clean out all the sink and tub drains when Sharon came in and told him that her car wouldn't start. Phil went out and looked under the hood as his wife turned the key. The clicking sound told him the battery was dead. He offered to give her a ride to the food pantry and then go to the automotive store to get a battery.

As they pulled up to the front door, Adele Sherman, a woman they knew from church, ran over to the car.

"We're short two volunteers this morning." She smiled at Phil. "Any chance you could give us a couple of hours this morning, Phil? We could really use a strong guy."

"Well, I don't know. I mean, how will I know what to do?" he said.

"Don't worry about that," she replied. "There are several bossy women ready to direct you. You look highly trainable to me." With that, she laughed, and Phil relaxed.

He spent the next three hours in the back room, filling boxes with groceries from lists. Peanut butter, canned soups, boxes of macaroni and cheese, toothpaste, and diapers flew off the shelves, into the boxes, and out the door. When Phil had a moment to breathe, he looked through the doorway to the pickup area. He was amazed at how many people got their food from this source. Mothers with babies and toddlers, men and women of all ages, some about his age. He wondered what stories he'd hear if he asked what had led them to need to use this charity.

When he and Sharon got home, he told her he'd like to do it again.

"I'm sure they'd love to have you. Adele told me you were a huge help. They're open Monday and Thursday. You could do just Mondays since that's the day I do the books."

"No, two days would be good. Can you let Adele know for me, please?"

A month later, Phil finished his Thursday shift at the food pantry and said goodbye to his bossy lady friends. He hadn't realized it was raining out, and he pulled his jacket over his head and ran to his car. He stopped at a red light in the center of town and saw a young couple waiting to cross. They wore light jackets, not sufficient for a day like this, Phil thought. They shared one misshapen umbrella, and each carried two bags of groceries from the food pantry. Phil opened the window on the passenger side and spoke to them.

"Hey, I see you're coming from the pantry. I work there in the back room. Can I give you a lift somewhere?"

The couple looked at him uncertainly, and then it starting pouring. Phil reached over and pushed open the door. "Get in, get in. You'll get soaked."

The man shut the front door, struggled to close the umbrella, and then got in the back with the woman.

"Hi, I'm Phil," he said, turning to shake their hands. "This rain came out of nowhere. Not a drop when I went in this morning. Where can I take you?"

The man said they lived about two miles away, just off the main road.

"No car?" Phil asked.

"No car." The man shook his head. "I'm Mike and this is my girlfriend, Tiffany. Thanks a lot for doing this, man."

Phil wanted to know where they were from. Did they have jobs? Why couldn't they afford groceries? How did they manage in a small town without a car? But he knew it was none of his business and he was quiet as they drove the two miles.

"Right here is good," Mike said, pointing to a sad-looking apartment building. "Thanks a lot. Phil, did you say?"

Phil nodded. "Anytime, Mike. Wait." Phil pulled a piece of paper and a pen out of the console and wrote his name and number on it. "This is my cellphone number. If the weather's bad, give me a call and I can give you a lift. This is a long walk carrying grocery bags."

"Thanks, man," Mike said.

Tiffany thanked him in a small voice, and they hoisted their bags and made a run for it. When they reached the shelter of the awning over the front door, they turned and waved. Phil waved back.

When he got home, he found Sharon putting lunch on the table.

"How was your morning?" she asked.

"Good. I gave a couple a ride home from the food pantry. They live two miles away and it was pouring out. They would've been drenched to the skin if I hadn't picked them up."

"What were their names?" Sharon asked.

"Mike and Tiffany. Young couple. Young and skinny. Do you know them?"

"I know who they are. They lost everything in a house fire over in Lowell. They're just getting back on their feet."

"Oh, that's tough. Poor kids." Phil sat down and took a bite of his sandwich. "I wonder if there are any other folks who need transportation. Maybe I'd be more helpful to people if I gave rides rather than filling orders."

"There are several people who walk quite a long way to get there. You know, there's an old van that's used to pick up food from the food bank sometimes. Why don't you suggest this to Adele and see if you could use the van? It was so good of you to help that couple today, Phil. I'm proud of you."

"Thanks," he said, pleased at the compliment. "I'm going to call Adele right after lunch."

After he'd talked to Adele, he headed for his recliner but then thought better of it. "The rain's stopped," he told his wife. "I'm going to go down and have a look at that van. Adele says she thinks it needs some work. I'll be back in an hour or so." He kissed her cheek as he left.

Sharon watched him go, striding purposefully, a small smile on his face. It seemed that Phil had found his rhythm at last.

HAIKUS
Annette Ermini

Old New England stones

Bridging the past and present

Earth's timeless heirlooms

A gift from nature—

Sunrise over the meadow

Colors in the sky

DECIDUOUS

Laurie Rosen

In North Hollow we know
it usually happens this way.
September meanders.
A solitary maple

in Harold's meadow
transforms red before we detect
any changes in the canopies
hovering the Hollow's dirt roads.

The air chills. In creeps
October. Kaleidoscopic
colors stain the Hollow's sky
while the maple in the meadow

taunts us, poised
leafless and alone.
But this year September
does not stroll slowly,

October doesn't slink in.
Autumn explodes all at once.
Orange, yellow, red swirl
above our heads, below our feet.

An urgency floods
the cool air.
Winter's icy breath
impatiently lurks,

ready to pounce, to bury
us permanently under
isolation and gloom.
The vernal awakening

will not occur
for a long while.
We tell ourselves,
it sometimes happens

this way, too.

Previously appeared in Uproar, *from The Lawrence House Center for the Arts Oct, 2021*

THE LONG VIEW
Michael Young

Greener Pastures

GRASS

An Anti-Pastoral
Fred Gerhard

"We're here!" shout the crocuses,
"Right where you left us
last year!" to the mumbling grass
trying to doze.

"We're purple and yellow and white!"
They blaze from the lawn.
The grass, beige, deranged, and matted
stifles a wispy yawn.

"We're the crocuses!" In unison
they lift their bright throats.
The grass manages reply in a raspy tone,
"Tomorrow, my friends, you might note

you crocuses will be but green leaves
as your petals parch and pass.
And we will bid you not to grieve.
But welcome you too, as grass."

MY GRANDFATHER'S LILTING
James Metcalf

In the summer of 1946, when I was six years old, my grandfather's home was a memory, and his mother and father, Margaret and John, had passed and were buried in the new Quabbin Park Cemetery. But I still remember bouncing on my grandfather's knee at the Quabbin Reservoir lookout, which faced the former location of the town of Enfield. When I visited, we sat on the bench, and he would tell me stories. He pointed in different directions, describing how it looked before the valley was flooded to create the Quabbin Reservoir.

"Over yonder stood my mother's favorite pasture ringed with rock walls," he said as though he could still see them. "The rock walls and open pastures reminded her of her home in Ireland."

His applewood pipe was always in his mouth, held there by a big wrapping of linen thread around the mouthpiece. I can still hear his voice gently rising and pleasantly falling with musical notes. It is known as lilting and was passed down from generation to generation in his Irish heritage.

Diddly – dee, diddly – do, riddly – diddly – dum – dee - do

"Everyone calls you Pa. Is that your real name?"

"To you, it's Grampa, but my mother named me John Kennedy after my father. You were named after my brother James, who settled over in Warren."

"Really? Can we visit him sometime? Did you have other brothers?"

"I have two brothers and one older sister, who stayed in Ireland. My mother's name was Margaret Anne Kennedy Metcalf. We were all born in County Armagh, Ireland, on a beautiful green farm— as green as this garden, but a little bigger."

"How big? What did you grow? Did you have any cows and horses?"

"Slow down, little Jim. I'll tell you all about the farm. We grew flax, which is made into linen for tablecloths. The farm was owned by my grandparents, who had sixteen children, including my mother, Margaret, who was born in 1844."

"Sixteen!" I could hardly believe it.

"That's right. But of the sixteen, only five survived childhood," he said. "Irish families were expected to give birth to one a year, but life was so hard that many died at birth or from disease or accidents."

"That's sad."

"Ah, sad it is. But my mother, Margaret, was fortunate because she had a brother, Robinson, ten years older than her, who she idolized. They say my mother was a beautiful yellow-haired little girl who loved to follow her older brother, Robinson, across the green pastures. Most folks gave her the nickname Robie's Shadow because you never saw one without the other. My mother had two younger brothers, William and Peter, twins one year younger than her. Their mother, also named Margaret, like my mother, was so protective of the twins that my mother had no other choice than to tie herself to Robinson."

I laughed while my grandfather tapped his pipe against the bench to clean the bowl.

"Those Kennedy kids lived through the Irish Potato Famine of 1845 to 1852. Potatoes were the primary food, rotting in the fields from a disease. So many people starved during that time. Farmers who sold potatoes lost their homes and farms because they could not pay rent to the English landlords who owned most of Ireland."

"What did they do?"

"Many men, women, and children tried to survive by begging or working by building roads and stone walls, which were given the name of famine walls. Their pay was meager and often came in food rations that were so small that they could not even feed workers' families. Many died, others became beggars or thieves, and those who could raise the price of ship passage escaped to other countries."

"Wow."

"The Kennedy farm was barely able to survive. Even though the potato crop rotted, a small kitchen garden provided vegetables. They grew flax and sold it to a large linen mill in Belfast, which provided meager money to feed the family."

"That was lucky for them."

"Rightly so. This was also the case with many families in Northern Ireland who did not tie their livelihood just to potatoes. Fortunately, these farmers shared what they could with the beggars and famine wall builders. Robinson and Margaret carried water and some vegetables to the starving workers. The people receiving these gestures of kindness were grateful and considered young Margaret, the blond girl walking with her older brother, an angel."

"An angel without wings," I piped up.

"Yes. But with a golden halo of blond curls. The famine took its toll on thousands of homeless roaming the country looking for food and shelter. Like their neighbors, the Kennedy family shared what they could with those knocking at their door. Margaret continued to follow Robinson, helping others. However, their primary job was working in their flax fields, weeding and harvesting the blue flowered stalks."

"That sounds like hard work."

"That it was. Flax required much hand work before being sold to the linen factory," My grandfather explained. "First, the flower seed pods had to be removed by pulling handfuls of plants over a series of nails to break the pods loose. The seed pods had to be broken open to save seeds for next year's planting of flax. Then, the two-foot stalks were tied in bundles and soaked in a brook to soften the outer layers. This task required walking over the bundles to sink them, then applying large rocks to keep them underwater."

"That sounds like fun."

"Ah, well, after checking for the correct tenderness of the stalks, the bundles were removed to dry by the sun in one of the rock-walled pastures. The final step was to rake the bundle of stalks across needle boards to remove the outer skins. This was a dusty, dirty job which was better done on breezy days to cut down on the breathing of the dust."

"I'm glad I don't have to do all that."

"It was mostly the job of older children as fathers worked in the linen mill, and their mother cared for the two younger children. But, as Robinson got older, his father got him a job as a helper in the Belfast linen mill, processing flax plants into yarn woven into linen cloth. When he was not at the mill, he worked on the farm alongside Margaret, who grew into a young woman while teaching her younger brothers the tasks required on the farm. The famine was ending and there were fewer homeless, allowing Margaret more time to enjoy the view across the pasture from atop the high stone walls."

"What do you think she thought about?"

"Maybe she thought about her future. One day, Robinson brought home a friend, John Metcalf, from the mill to help him repair a rake used to smooth the ground for planting. John Metcalf was two years older than Margaret, but there was definitely a spark between the two teenagers. John accompanied Robinson on these home visits more often, and there was always time for Margaret and John to walk the fields or sit together on that high wall. After a time, the relationship turned into a marriage proposal, which her father approved, followed by an Irish wedding on December 7, 1864, in Milltown, county of Armagh. Her brothers celebrated the marriage of their only sister well into the following day."

"That must have been some party!"

"That it was. Afterward, John and Margaret stayed on the farm in a small building the family built for them. Margaret delivered their first child, a girl named Margaret Ann Metcalf, after her mother. John and Margaret had three more children who were unfortunately stillborn. It was devastating to the family. However, in 1877, I, John Kennedy Metcalf, was born, followed by my brother Robert in 1881 and James in 1883."

"Yay!"

"Yay, indeed. The family was complete, but now a longing for a better life was spreading across families, driven by letters describing great living and working conditions from people who emigrated to countries like Canada, the United States, and Australia during the famine."

"So, did they come to America then?"

"Well, some did. The second industrial revolution was beginning, and towns like Manchester, Connecticut, became the center of this new revolution, with the Cheney Brothers Silk Mill, advertised as the world's largest silk manufacturer, and the Hillard Woolen Mill, the first wool cloth mill in the United States. These companies and others advertised worldwide for experienced weavers and cloth processors."

"They were brave."

John and Robinson caught the adventure bug and planned to emigrate, then relocate their families once they settled. But there would be time apart. So, the excitement was mixed with worry about the voyage and the separation of loved ones. Nevertheless, John and

Robinson emigrated to Connecticut to work as weavers in the Cheney Mill in 1886."

"So how did they end up in the Swift River Valley?"

"Soon, mills in the Swift River Valley of Western Massachusetts began advertising for skilled weavers. This enticed my father and Robinson to accept positions in Enfield because, as they said in their letters home, this valley is as beautiful as Ireland, with large green pastures circled with perfect stone walls."

"When did you come to America?"

"With some advice from her husband and brother, my mother purchased four Steerage passage tickets to New York City departing from Glasgow, Scotland, aboard the steamship *Devonia* on March 31, 1887. He and Robinson were to meet them. The trip was scheduled to take sixteen days, but this passage arrived on April 12, three days early. The first couple of days were filled with sea sickness and bucket brigades to the ship's stern. After that, it was dull, so people entertained each other with lilting."

Diddly – dee, diddly – do, riddily – diddly – dum – dee - do

"It was accompanied by Irish step dancing. My mother was traveling with me, the oldest at ten, along with Robert, age six, and James, age four. Our mother was a good singer, especially putting us to sleep with her lullabies, but now she learned lilting from other passengers, which we also practiced with our mother. Since we arrived in New York three days early, we worried about where we would stay while waiting for our father, but Irish luck caused our father to anticipate an early arrival, and he was waiting for us upon arriving in New York. We went to the railroad station and waited for the next train headed in the direction of Enfield. Our waiting was one long hug with Father."

"Was this before the reservoir, when the fields were still open, and the stone walls bordered them?"

"Yes, my mother could not get over how beautiful the Swift River Valley and our new home were. She kept saying. "Are we still in Armagh?" The friends of Father and Uncle Robinson welcomed us with a party of fresh food, music, and dancing."

Diddly – dee, diddly – do, riddly – diddly – dum – dee - do

"What a welcome!" My eyes sparkled with the thought.

"After unpacking, we explored our neighborhood, town, and valley. The summer began, allowing us to start a garden, explore, and fish for the first time in the clear Swift River. The next few years were our happiest ever, with Mother and Father taking us on walks and picnics to view the open pastures and perfect stone walls surrounding the green fields. A new generation of American Irish began in this valley, moving across other states, always celebrating the green pastures and stone walls with stories and lilting."

Diddly — dee, diddly — do, riddly — diddly — dum — dee - do

My grandfather's voice still lilts in my memory all these years later.

Diddly — dee, diddly — do, riddly — diddly — dum — dee - do

STONE HEDGE

Steven Michaels

Century old wisdom tells us
fences make good neighbors.
As I walk through the valleys
of old New England villages
I see the sage's advice
on antiquated display.
Stone structures built
for *your* Puritanical protection
Never realizing what was at "stake"
separation, anxiety
social impediments
fortified by paranoia
such that Tituba be hanged
Proctors be pariahs
while the righteous rectify
societal norms
safely ensconced
behind the stonework.
Beware the third nipple
putting cracks in your foundation.
At Stone Hedge
we will purify
the sinner and the strange
lay them out upon the slab
carve out the heart of our village
sacrifice our human-ity
to appease our own image
or
we could *pray*
that our past remains inside the stone
then turn it over so that
no walls remain.

THE TURKEY PRINT
Diane Hinckley

[In the early nineteenth century, footprints in Connecticut Valley sandstone were believed to be those of extinct birds. We now know that they were put down by dinosaurs.]

Pausing by the stone wall at the bottom of Spaulding Hill, Miss Eliza Merrifield eyed the imprint in one of the boulders. The sandstone seemed out of place among the more durable blocks in the wall. She supposed the rock with its giant footprint might be meant as a decoration, though such frivolity would be unusual among the farmers of western Massachusetts.

"That's the turkey footprint," chirped Aurelia Spaulding, her star pupil and companion on this walk.

"It must have been a rather large gobbler," joked Miss Merrifield. "Doctor Edward Pritchard of Amherst College tells us that these huge prints were put down by giant birds, now extinct. Their footprints are left to us because the giants were caught up in a cataclysm they were unable to escape. They took their last walk in the mud and were seen no more."

"That's what Father says, complete with the cataclysm part," replied the precocious child, "but everyone just calls it the turkey print. Father says it doesn't matter that we know different because there's people that have to know it as the turkey print."

"It's 'people who.' Child, whatever are you talking about?"

"Father says there's things some people need to know and things some people need not to know."

"It's 'there are,' not 'there's,' and you are being mysterious." Miss Merrifield had often experienced unease around young Aurelia, who always seemed on the verge of blurting out some secret.

The teacher and her pupil turned up the dusty drive toward the Spaulding house. Miss Merrifield hoped that Aurelia's father would be at home so she could broach the subject of his daughter's future. In a few years, the child would be a perfect candidate for matriculation at the Mount Holyoke Female Seminary, where she might learn enough to take up teaching, should life put her in need of earning a living, and Miss Merrifield wanted to start softening up the girl's parent.

As a widower—a condition acquired under notoriously murky circumstances—with only one child, he might not wish Aurelia to leave his household before marriage. She would save him the expense of a housekeeper.

Speculation over the darkly enigmatic but eligible Mr. Spaulding had instigated a Lord Byron craze among the local maidens, who had also managed to wear out the library's copy of *Jane Eyre*. Strangely, these young ladies were the only local people willing to talk about Mr. Spaulding or his house, which they confided, eyes wide, was a "house of secrets."

One evening, over a cup of cider, Aurelia's Aunt Augusta had revealed to Miss Merrifield that, just as in a silly novel, her brother-in-law really had been disappointed in love, by her own sister, Aurelia's mother. "Flora ran off with an itinerant farm hand, and later we got word from Vermont that she'd died. I think she ran off because she felt she needed to escape, but didn't know from what."

Miss Merrifield could have waited to bring up the topic of Miss Lyon's seminary, but she feared that she would be away from Massachusetts as early as next spring. She could teach in the Far West just as well as she could here, and the glut of men in the West might enable her to escape spinsterhood.

Although her room at Aurelia's aunt's house was pleasant, as was Aurelia's aunt, and—to a lesser degree—Aurelia's uncle, Miss Merrifield longed for a household of her own. She had no special ties to the Connecticut Valley, having come originally from Lowell. She had arrived in the area to study at the seminary and found work in the Valley upon graduation.

When Aurelia's Aunt Augusta learned of Miss Merrifield's mission to her brother-in-law's house, she put that evening's pie in a basket as a gift. Miss Merrifield was disappointed because she'd been looking forward to the pie, but at the same time she liked the idea of arriving with a present to oil the wheels of persuasion. At any rate, it was September, a time when apple pies were frequently on the table, so there was no use feeling deprived.

She was concerned, however, when she heard Augusta whisper to Aurelia about "visitors on the way" to her father's house. Miss Merrifield hoped that, whoever they were, they would hold off arriving until she'd made her case.

As the two trudged up the hill, Miss Merrifield thought about the footprint weathering in the stone wall. If Mr. Spaulding was anything like Aurelia's stern, closed-mouth uncle, she would abstain from recommending that the rock be carried to a museum. Aurelia's education was her priority.

Aurelia ran to open the farmhouse door for Miss Merrifield, who was holding the basket, thus forcing the teacher to stride right into Mr. Spaulding's house without a warning.

Two figures jumped up from the shadowy area beside the hearth. They were thin and plainly dressed and appeared terrified.

"Don't be scared," said Aurelia. "We brought a pie."

Neither of the strangers spoke. The darkness of the room obscured their features, though from their dress it was plain that one was a man and the other was a woman.

"I see you found the turkey print," said Aurelia to the couple. "Is Father around?"

Just then, Mr. Spaulding walked into the room. "Aurelia," he demanded in a voice like iron. "Who is your guest?"

Aurelia stood speechless, obviously frightened that she had done something wrong. She plainly knew what that something was.

When Miss Merrifield got a closer look at the young couple, she understood the secret this house had been keeping. She spoke boldly, introducing herself as Aurelia's teacher. "Mr. Spaulding, we have brought a pie," she said, "for you and your guests."

Mr. Spaulding stared hard at her, then seemed to relax, as though her frank look had brought him to an understanding of her character. "Perhaps you would partake of some cider, Miss Merrifield," he said. "You might enjoy the story my guests have to tell. They arrived sooner than I'd expected, having been forced to leave Worcester in a hurry."

"A slave catcher came in on the train," said the young man.

Titus, as the man was called, and his wife, Marcy, had escaped from a plantation in Virginia and followed the Underground Railroad all the way to Massachusetts, where they learned of the stone wall with the giant footprint. They'd had some close calls along the way, now that slave catchers roamed the North as well as the South. A person could be captured as far north as New England and sent back into slavery.

"Fugitive Slave Act," spat Mr. Spaulding.

As Miss Merrifield was leaving with the now empty basket, she found her chance to bring up the topic of Aurelia's future. Mr. Spaulding seemed amenable and declined to insult her by extracting a promise of secrecy concerning his visitors. Instead, he told her she was welcome at any time.

As she walked past the "turkey print," Miss Merrifield pondered her own future and thought she might want to serve another year in the Valley after all. There was no use escaping if you didn't know what you were escaping from.

FREEPORT

Thom Anthony

I see in the news that art
hangs unknown, warehoused
in Switzerland by those who
want to own but never
need to see it.

Tax shelter art,
commodity art; I am puzzled
by the relationship. If I don't
see it now, then how shall
I miss it? Because it exists,
knowing of it is a worry.

Art swells with illumination.
Shadows lengthen in time
till finally it is lost—a repository
of inspiration and beauty hard
and soft, imprisoned by life,
blinded to stars and lights and the
landscapes of desires.

I miss fantastic hands
that buff to a brilliant shine.
Today art stares from a
darkened closet where
art can only imagine
each other's eyes.

I should be there to
listen; to hear the putdowns,
sobs and laughter—
art preening and celebrating
vanity and eternity.

In the fastness of a Swiss
bunker, I ask, is it art
if it is unseen? Why save
the world's greatest wines
and not drink them?

A 100-year-old wine sleeps
restlessly, outliving memory.
Wine needs attention.
Art only written about is
vulnerable to the worst
imagination and worshipped
by accountants whose
attention never catches more
than a glimpse from the page.
Art must spring from a wall,
leap from its cage and
mingle with the crowds.
We must shake its hand
ask after the family.

What I imagine is not an
impressionist's pasture,
or another idle flower by
Monet. I want to imagine
the atelier, the agony and
crushing exercise of birth.

They are shuttered from me.
I will never know them. I
want to stumble over Pablo
at the beach, or Louise, Gustav
Franz, and Vincent. I want to
walk an August farm in
Arles and talk about light.

I want to hear Diego and
Frida arguing technique
outside the dark storeroom,
where van Rijn and Velasquez leap borders
and languages to reason why.

They will always know,
I never will—a warehouse is a tomb.
where dark unfeeling walls cannot see
and whispers have no sound.
Wealth is never mentioned when
there is no price. Creation has no
bottom line, but the counters do

Braque and Brueghel,
Claudel and Caravaggio,
Corbet and Corot,
Hassam and Angelico
Georges and Gaugin—
voices in my imagination.
They know the answers,
I never will. Better they had
never lived, or burned and
vanished from our sight,
lest they be reinspired,
for me to see what might have been.

LETTERS FROM
PRESCOTT PINE GROVE CEMETERY
Karen Traub

The first time I visited the Swift River Museum in New Salem a number of years ago, I became curious to learn more about the Prescott 1895 Signature Quilt hanging on the stairway of the Whitaker Clary House. Although I have not yet discovered how it found its way to the Hitchcock Chair Museum in Connecticut, research led me to understand that most of the fifty names embroidered on the quilt were people who lived around North Prescott and Atkinson Hollow. Many were members of the Prescott Golden Rule Grange, Pine Grove Cemetery, and Prescott Historical Society.

Proceeds from the sale of the Pine Grove Cemetery to the Water Commission paid for the land where the Prescott Methodist Episcopal church was moved in 1942, after being purchased by the Historical Society for five dollars, to serve as a museum. The church was moved a second time to its current site and serves as part of the Swift River Valley Historical Society.

Prescott, along with Dana, Enfield and Greenwich, were the towns sacrificed to create a reservoir providing water to the city of Boston in the early nineteenth century. Through birth, marriage, death records, photographs, newspaper articles, letters, and legal documents, I've gotten to know some of the townspeople well enough to imagine how a correspondence with them might go.

February 14, 2025

To Whom It May Concern,

We, the undersigned representing the Society of the Pine Grove Cemetery, dead these many years, do hereby grant permission to tell our story; to share the ins and outs, ups and downs, loves and losses of a small New England town that met a sad end, in order to keep our memories alive and perhaps help the current generation understand the benefits of pulling together to get through hard times.

Through the universe on behalf of the spirits of the Prescott Pine Grove Cemetery Association,

Lillie B. Coolidge and Henry White

~~~~~~~~~~~~~~~~~~~~~~~

February 18, 2025

Dear Ms. Traub,

Since you have been so eagerly researching my family and neighbors in your quest to know who made the signature quilt, I thought I'd take this opportunity to speak to you directly via the Open Spirit Channel. My name is Ellis White. I was born in 1814 and died in1909. Quite a few of my family contributed to the quilt and we are also among those who helped establish the Pine Grove Cemetery Society in 1880. We've enjoyed watching you discover how we were related to each other and appreciate your efforts to keep our memories alive.

Hannah Alma Pierce was my beloved wife and we had two sons, Anson and Josiah. You were surprised and wondered why Alma and I each had our own quilt square ((Mr Ellis White-row 10 square 1, Mrs. E. White-row 3 square 5).

Anson married Mary Long and they were the parents of Henry White with whom you are acquainted from his work with the Historical Society. That neither of them has a square in the quilt leads you to wonder whether they might in fact have been recipients of the quilt. We won't spoil the mystery.

Our grandaughters Flossy and Cora, toddlers at the time, each had their own square, although their brother Crighton wasn't born in time to get one. (Flossy White- row 11 square 1 and Cora White- Row 10 square 4). Their parents, Josiah and Nellie (Haskins) each has a square (Mr. J. E. White-row1 square1, and Mrs. J.E. White- row 4 square 4) instead of sharing one.

My Alma's brother was Daniel Pierce who you saw in a family photograph and have been saying to people "looks like a cross between a young Jerry Garcia and a muppet." He certainly did have a lot of long thick black hair blending into his full bushy beard. Daniel was what we call a jack of all trades, and he had a hunger to live life to its fullest. He was a storyteller who had traveled the world through books. He shared his curiosity and wonder with his children, whether showing them how a magnifying glass can start a fire or catching lightning bugs in a jar. Daniel lived on the Pierce farm with his wife Ellen (row 7 square 4) and their six children. You are familiar with the youngest, that imp who was always asking questions and grew into a respected historian, and preserver of our memories- Lillie Belle (row 11 square 2). I know it's confusing that there were Pierces and Peirces and that Ellen was both, being born a Peirce and married to a Pierce. We laughed and clapped our hands sharing your delight when you learned that Lillie Belle was descended from both Appleton "Prayin' App" Pierce, and Appleton "Swearin' App" Peirce.

As you have read in Lillie's outstanding book "The History of Prescott," Pine Grove Cemetery was about halfway between Atkinson Hollow and North Prescott. Now, it wasn't any big deal but I donated the land and made the pickets for the fence around the cemetery. Everybody did their share. A group of us got together and formed a society of members who purchased plots for five dollars. We bought stone posts from Joseph Stone for 2 shillings apiece. Daniel Pierce and others pitched in to put the posts and fence up.

While I have your kind attention, I want to make sure that someone keeps track of the intention of our children and grandchildren who bore the burden of overseeing the removal of our bodies from the Pine Grove cemetery in 1942, to erect a monument from the stone posts salvaged and stored away long ago.

In closing, I want to thank you for taking an interest in the people of Prescott and know that we are standing by to help and cheer you on in telling our stories.

Sincerely,
Ellis White

~~~~~~~~~~~~~~~~~~~~~~~~~

February 25, 2025

Dear Henry White,

I want to thank you and the other members of the Prescott Historical Society for saving the church to be used as a museum and archive, and for making my research a pleasure.

I liked you from the minute I saw a photograph of you as a young boy. I was going through a box of photos from Prescott looking for members of the Berry family when I came across one of you looking like a forlorn Little Lord Fauntleroy telegraphing, "I'm doing my best to stand straight like a soldier with my arm across the back of a chair to keep my balance in these pointy-toed shoes that hurt my feet." In the box of photos, there was also one of you as an infant and an older man, and always your face is a pleasant one with an inscrutable expression, neither a smile nor frown, a guileless face whose owner lived a life dedicated to his community.

I am only now learning about your connection to the Prescott Signature Quilt, the Historical Society, Grange and Pine Hill Cemetery.

I read your father Anson's obituary and learned you were a popular letter carrier. Hats off to a rural bringing of news and letters to loved ones far away. It mentions your involvement with the Masons and

Legionnaires, but having been written in 1938 did not know you would go on to be the president of Prescott Historical Society.

Please assure your family and neighbors that I'll give it my best shot to see that they are not forgotten.

With admiration and appreciation,
Karen

~~~~~~~~~~~~~~~~~~~~~~~~~

February 26, 2025

Dear Karen,

Please allow me to introduce myself. I am Dr. Walter A. Clark of Atkinson Hollow. I was Prescott's last medical doctor and the last person to run the Atkinson tavern which I often visit in its current location at Storrowton Village at the Big E in West Springfield. As you can imagine, running a tavern without electricity wasn't easy. I'm glad to see they have made some upgrades over the last hundred years.

My wife was the former Verena Gloor whom I met while in Switzerland and yes, you are correct that her initials, V.C. (row 1 square 4) are the ones which Helen Canney in researching the quilt in the 1980's could not identify. Helen was related to many people on the quilt but not us. Verena and I had no children.

In the photo you found in the archive which includes Daniel, Ellen, myself, and Lillie Pierce, I am the guy you said looks like Rasputin. Sure, my long black beard was unusual for a man at the turn of the twentieth century and people said my eyes were deep dark and hypnotic like a snake, where you can't look away. Whether I was a genius or charlatan, someone you'd enjoy a game of cards with or steer clear of, you can only speculate. Like you, I didn't always fit in and the townspeople considered me to be somewhere between eccentric and completely nuts. Church people were afraid of me but came to me for help when they were hurt or ill.

You wonder if I was a follower of Spiritualism which professed to cross the veil in communication beyond the grave and was big around here in the early 20th century - well, I am writing to you so there's your answer.

I hope people will remember me for who I loved and how I lived; whose lives I touched or even saved, the places I've seen and the books I've read, the music, dances at the Grange hall, my courtship and deep abiding love and partnership with Verena, how a few of us stayed as long as we could and fought with all our might to keep our land. The loss extended over a dozen years when the people of Prescott begged only for it to be over quickly. Try to imagine the parade of packed-up cars and trucks leaving home, the sad letters from near and far, and whose father or grandfather said he'd rather die than leave his home, and did.

I'd rather be remembered for how I lived than how I died which was, as you read in the archive "found dead September 26, 1930 in his home at 51 Winter Street in Athol by his nephew Warren Tollman with whom he lived."

You should have seen how people pulled together and were torn apart when the Commonwealth of Massachusetts flooded our valley to make a reservoir. In a small town everybody knows, for better or worse, everybody else's business, who is sick or dying, getting married or having an affair, goes to which or no church. These same people pull together in hard times because that's the only way forward.

Before I close, please take note that it is the job of historical fiction to take the reader back in time, introduce people, places and things to make history come alive and to represent the people with the best intention. You have very little information about me and my wife, Verena Gloor, and aren't you just dying to know the nature of our relationship- well, you will just have to make it up. Make me Rasputin if that will make the story better, as long as you portray me with respectful intention. I hope our messages from the past might offer some wisdom for the future.

Please keep in touch.

Yours Truly,
Dr. Walter A. Clark

~~~~~~~~~~~~~~~~~~~~~~~

Dear Mrs. Traub,

I am Warren Whipple and I rebuilt the North Prescott store in 1894 after LK Baker was burned out a second time. Later, it was Currier's when Helen Canney's grandfather Frank J. Currier bought it. It was Wheeler's in the end, and that's where Prescott's last town meeting was held. The name "H.V. Whipple" as it occurs in the 1895 quilt Row 8 Square 2, is my wife Hattie, maiden name Vorce. I wanted you to know that.

Yours truly,
Warren Whipple

~~~~~~~~~~~~~~~~~~~~~~~

Dear Spirit Friend Karen,

Sorry for busting in here with my own agenda when I'm not a member of any society but you simply must disassociate my name with that of my mother's husband Nymphas Stacy. He was a respected man in Prescott and I am recorded by history as "notorious" because I refused to adhere to the town's notion of a good girl.

I understand you have the highest regard for renowned Quabbin Historial J.R. Greene who tells my story in his book, "Strange Tales from Old Quabbin." I was called by many names in my time and "notorious" was the least of them. But if my stepfather had anything to do with my downfall or if his name belied his own proclivities, believe me, you don't want to know the details. In the 1800s women couldn't vote or own property. We, in fact, WERE property, so you tell Mr. Greene there's something to say for a woman making a living even if the townspeople or the laws don't approve.

When liquor was illegal, we drank it anyway. Folks like to have a beer after a hard day's work; you know that from your days bartending at the Shutesbury Athletic Club. Remember how surprised you were when someone explained to you what a body shot is? Ha! I know you saw and heard a thing or two and met people at the bar that you never did when you were a trustee at the library.

You're lucky to live in a time when terms like "fallen woman," "house of ill repute," and "ladies of the night," are no longer used by people proclaiming moral superiority. Some people are really hung up on that Adam and Eve story and I feel bad for the women stuck in abusive marriages who blame themselves because of Eve taking a bite of the apple of knowledge. I'm glad to see that sex workers are finally organizing for their rights. Rock on modern women!

J.R. Greene was right that I was hauled before the court eleven times between 1847 and 1866 for selling illegal liquor and sex. It's true my son Wilson was born just seven months after I married that no-good two-timing horse thief Warren Hunt. Right after our second son was born, Hunt was convicted of adultery with the spinster Mary Felton. A divorce was granted for my willful and utter desertion of him. I would have done anything to get rid of that deadbeat.

There were more people arrested for bigamy in those days than there are today, and when I married Oliver Davis Jr. in 1848, I was hauled in on polygamy charges. After being acquitted, they trumped up a charge of "lewd and lascivious cohabitation" with my husband. I appealed and won. I also was acquitted when that fool from Petersham got himself shot at my establishment.

Go ahead and repeat the story of the stolen horse harness being found in my bed. Feel free to embellish the details, the wilder the better. It's true I was arrested and escaped from the warden's house in my nightgown in the middle of the night. That's what he got for not putting me in jail proper just because it was over-filled with men.

My reputation spread far and wide and in an editorial one of my admirers wrote: "She wouldn't have been afraid of fifty men." Oh, did we have a good laugh when the jailer offered a fifty-dollar reward for my capture. I paid a kid five bucks to turn me in and kept the other forty-five..

I saw a meme on the ghostly interweb that said "Well-behaved women rarely make history." Please let that be the answer to the story in J.R. Greene's book.

Your friend,
The Notorious Betsy Hunt

~~~~~~~~~~~~~~~~~~~~~~~

February 27, 2025

Dear Karen,

Thank you for taking an interest in my life and that of my family and community who lived around the west branch of the Swift River. As you know, like you were one hundred years after me, I was a trustee at the M. N. Spear Memorial Library in Shutesbury. I was also a school teacher in Shutesbury, Prescott, and eventually Springfield after Herbert died and my sister Bessie and I moved away from home.

Herbert and I were only married four years when he died. We were both in our mid-forties and neither of us had ever married. As you know, there are many types of love from courtly to familial, to bonds of deep mutual respect. Herbert's heart failed him and he was buried in Pine Grove cemetery. My name and birth date were already carved into his stone when we got word that all the bodies were to be dug up and moved. It was too sad for words to sign the papers to move my mother, father, husband and friends to the Quabbin cemetery, but someone had to do it. I will answer your question as to why a member of the Lura Club (we had over a thousand members from around the world named Lura) signed my name Laura on the Water Commission photograph. It was a legal document and that was my legal name. Please continue to call me Lura as that is what my friends called me.

Now, let's talk about happier times. We were as tickled as you were that Bessie chaired the cake and ice cream committee at the grange. What good times we had! In the '80s and '90s we would go to dances every two weeks during the winter months at the Prescott Grange Hall. Dr. Clark played his violin and Waldo Peirce would call the dances like the Portland Fancy. I can still hear his rhythmic voice booming through the hall, "Join hands and swing eight, now head couple down the middle and around the outside." Carrie Wheeler played the organ and Dexter Wheelock played clarinet.

Of course because we lived in Shutesbury, Bessie and I didn't contribute squares to the Prescott signature quilt. Still, our cousins Annie (row 1 square 5), her brother Charlie's wife (Mrs. C.W. Berry row 3 square 1), and my sister-in-law Laura (Miss L.S. Peirce- row 5 square 5) who married Herbert's brother Allie, are in there. It was good that I went by the name Lura because otherwise we would have both been Laura Barnes!

It feels good knowing you are putting effort into making sure we are remembered and I'm glad to be in touch.

Your friend,
Lura Berry Barnes

~~~~~~~~~~~~~~~~~~~~~~~~

ACCIDENTAL ARCHAEOLOGY
Melissa Rossetti Folini

Pieces of clay pigeon.

Amber root beer bottle.

Pottery shard.

Shotgun shell.

Golf ball.

The woods I now walk where I once used to play,

and spend time with relatives visiting for the day,

over grew as I aged and lay silently waiting for me.

After many years away,

walks with a little dog on a recurring loop

have unearthed treasures that,

aside from memories and myself,

are all that remain of Saturday shoots

and Sunday dinners.

Those family members have long passed

but the signs that remain of that time,

decades later,

elicit a nostalgic smile.

ON A TRAIN FROM
BIRMINGHAM ENGLAND TO
GLASGOW SCOTLAND
LuAnn Thibodeau

ODE TO SAO MIGUEL, AZORES
Lorri Ventura

Ghosts of long-gone forebears
  Linger at the lagoons and calderas
And dance playfully in steam
  Above thermal pools and hot springs
Steadfast in their conviction
  That Heaven's celestial splendor
Pales next to Sao Miguel's beauty

Cows lumber along the same stone-studded paths
  Trod by their ancestors centuries ago
As they circle the emerald hollows of Sete Cidades
  Their hooves follow ancient trails
That hug the hills like pearl strands around a neck

The faces of Jesus and Mary
  Bob benevolently on the bows of the fishing boats
In the harbor at Ponta Delgada
  While exuberant geysers spray the sky above Furnas
And volcanic heat cooks cozido stew to perfection
  In underground pots planted as lovingly as rosebushes

If Heaven exists
  It floats in the middle of the Atlantic Ocean
As part of nine-island Azorean archipelago
  Sao Miguel!

ALL THAT IS MISSING
Thomas Reed Willemain

In days gone by, the scene he surveyed would have invited him to an effortless idyll. Ignore the break in the wall – jump the wall instead. Glide up and down the hills. Revel in the seductive undulations of the western Mass topography. Seductive because it always pulled his eyes away from the dangerous undulations of the local roads.

But that was then; now was different. The broken wall was not as important as his broken body. Too many hard falls followed by too many hard surgeries and hard recoveries. He could try to imagine jumping, but it would be like trying to imagine a bad dream. Not happening.

So he just stood still, turned slowly to take in the scene, and tried not to acknowledge the ramble he was not about to begin.

Uncomfortable with pondering his physical decline but not willing to walk away, he soon found a different reason to be where he was. He focused on the stonework and the particular way that the wall was topped. It was just like every stone wall he'd seen in the short months he'd lived with his wife in Lancashire. That town had more sheep than people, and of course the one pub was named "The Fleece".

Then it hit him. There was something missing in the vista before him, but it wasn't the missing section of wall. Where were all the sheep?

THE GRASSHOPPER
Cindy Boundy

The skates will not roll on the soft dirt
Unbuckle the straps and kick them of your shoes
Leave them by the gate

The grass in the big field
comes up and over your knees almost to your waist
If you stray off the path

Wandering amongst the tall stalks
Searching for a blade of grass
Thick enough to press between your thumbs
To make a whistle

With cupped hands
Catch a grasshopper
The green and yellow creature
With long antennae and folded legs

Brings good fortune
For all that is ahead
Open your palm, wide
Let it jump and fly away

Sunshine fills the field with warmth
The breeze is gentle on your face
A voice calls from the back porch,
"It's time to go"

LATE MIGRATION
Karen Durlach

Immersed in this benevolent Hitchcock
    black silhouettes punctuate my cloudless sky
    flapping   perching   cackling   chirping
    the annual migration
    flocks foraging, fluttering, fussing their way south
Before the neighbors built across the street
    they'd land in their thousands
    where now a splash of asphalt lies
    but still they come,
    readjust
    to only memory of meadow
Before that paving,
    before us,
    assuredly decades, centuries
    of predetermined flyway laid in their genes
    generations of birds passed just this way
    gathered   trading gossip   bonding
    leap-frogging branch to branch, tree to tree
Waves of dark bodies pause, pass on.

A battered old tree almost barkless now
    —but probably younger than this old trunk—
    leans over the stone wall,
    precarious
You can barely tell I raked our driveway
    oak leaves still hanging on
    still reluctantly falling
    still whispering down
    being blown back   up   about   from gathered piles
    tumbling across tarmac, littering the road
November 1st a late mixed flock swoops over
    chatters high
    cascades in unison
    some stop   circle back to a still-leafed tree
    dark bodies perching amidst crispy russet rustle

until their weight shakes more leaves loose
with simultaneous launch
Another wave passes   dapples the blue autumn.

Neck-tired from looking up,
I perch on a rock
just listen
hear all the spirits of eons
Birds who could blacken the skies.

EAST STREET CEMETERY, SEASONS OF A STONE WALL: A MEMOIR

Kimberly A Beckham

I have lived my entire life on East Street in a rural community with a charming small-town feel. I have always taken issue with calling my location "East Street." It is a lovely winding country road that stretches from the center of my town through farmland and woods to the center of the next town roughly seven miles southeast. It is a road, just wide enough for two vehicles and in some spots nearly gravel, in a community where front yards were once full of children playing ball and grandparents in rockers telling stories.

I knew from the start, some two hundred and a few years ago, I would not stray. Why would I? It is a beautiful gently rolling field surrounded by trees and fields. I have just one neighbor to my west. That home has changed hands from time to time – some owners more neighborly than others but all in all, I've been lucky. Lucky but for one thing. There is currently a rooster that crows throughout the day. I haven't yet decided if I am pleased about that or not, but I never did need much sleep. I have clear boundaries with all my neighbors. You might say I am the boundary setter.

I have had a full life and expect it to go on for many years. Perhaps it is too early for a memoir. What have I accomplished, after all?

In the spring of my life, after a plot of land was cleared for a very important town amenity, stones, rounded over time by Mother Earth and New England weather, were selected from area fields, clearing the way for farmers to grow crops and cows to meander and graze. They were brought to the plot of land in carts and barrows. Every inch of me was created carefully by loving hands and thoughtful hearts with an eye to the future, my own and theirs. I am connected to everyone and everything in this town. I have outlived many of the neighbors. I even miss a few of them.

My most important passion and life's work has never changed. Over the years, I have welcomed many friends and neighbors to stay here within my boundaries. They've all been very well behaved, for the most part. People visit often so I am never lonely. And when there are no visitors, I have the honor of hosting many species of both feathered and furry friends. Some stroll through looking for food, some fly over, others create homes. They enjoy the quiet as much as I do, giving the property a park-like atmosphere except for the untimely crowing from next door.

Throughout the summer of my life, I settled in. I felt strong and hearty, shaded by trees that took root near the small pond. Cattails danced, gently swaying in the breeze along a tiny creek that pinches the property like a belt at the waist. Every person who comes to stay on the property comes with their own story, some very imaginative, some humorous, some quite emotional. I never tire of them. I am practically surrounding a museum as well as a beautiful park full of friends and neighbors.

I expect my life's work to continue onward through the current century, though there are days I feel as though I may be reaching full capacity. I have worries about that. I try to set them aside because over the years I have learned that anxiety is good for no one, even me. I see people driving by me now heading for other locations as their final needs arise. I am not full yet, where are they going? It's the rooster, isn't it? He is chasing people away.

My health has been mostly good but on cold, damp New England days and nights I can feel the shifting that goes on in my stoney bones. My job has always been to set a boundary but as I age, I can feel the weakening beginning.

As I move into the autumn of my life, my appearance has changed, but whose hasn't? There is no lotion that can reverse this aging process for me. For example, there is a swamp, the origins of which I have always attributed to a family of beavers who moved into the area many decades ago. They built the tiniest lodge to house their family along a small creek in a field far behind me. Their descendants have moved on but their lodge and the resulting flooding created a swamp that has caused me some unsightly scarring along the edge of me to the north. I feel as though I am missing bits of myself, because I am, but I do my best to hold strong. Sometimes the water rises after heavy rains and seethes through me into the grass and around my guests saturating the ground. There is nothing I can do but wait until it lowers to assess the damage.

As I look forward to the winter of my life, I expect there will be some difficulties; not the snow so much as the ice. Ice can be dangerous and unforgiving. It moves in channels deep inside me, chilling me and forcing my bones apart in painfully slow and debilitating ways. Even long after the sun rises and does its best to remind us that spring is never far off, I can still feel its effects. The damage is done. You have seen the crumbling, haven't you? I can't hide it.

I have decided not to think about that because I will be fine. I am a survivor. I am still young, after all.

There are kind people who observe the effect of the forest along my eastern arm. Occasionally, a tree may need to be removed as their roots can be very pushy and bully me to distraction. Frankly I am afraid the town will someday notice my weaknesses and make decisions that will…I shudder to think. And I should not shudder as that always causes the smaller bits of me to shift.

As with all aging, it is out of my hands, so to speak. I will wake each morning to whatever the day brings. I will enjoy the tickles of the chipmunks and squirrels running along my arms as I stretch to hold on to this land. Earthbound, I will marvel as the birds, tiny sparrows and majestic osprey, as they soar overhead. I have a job to do and will keep doing it as long as I am allowed. I am not yet done.

Please come visit. I will see what I can do about that rooster.

BRITISH LANDSCAPES
Allan Fournier

We start in Scotland's Edinburgh
Or is it Edinboro?
The locals say it "Edinbra"
Or something else tomorrow

Rocky hills and rolling rills
And sheep all o'er the place
Old Town, New Town, castles, jewels
Sir Wallace, with blueface

Through the Borders, off we go
To wed at Gretna Green
Even if Mom, Dad say no
"Tie the knot" though just a teen

To Northern England, Vindolanda
Roman fortress site
Soldiers washed with olive oil
And lived in quarters tight

Next, medieval city York
With quaint and narrow streets
ABC[1], the Minster
And tasty ales and eats

Chester has old city walls
To keep out ye intruder
Charming shopping, houses, too
Victorian and Tudor

Cross into Wales, Llangollen
Aqueduct over a stream
Then tasty cakes and tea
Afternoon, not High or Cream!

Back again to Chester
Heard Town Crier give the news
Be careful of your shopping
Lest you get the pillory blues!

Next Bill the Bard's birthplace
Shakespeare's Stratford upon Avon
Enjoy the English countryside
His works, you can rave on

To Oxford we go next
It's University has flair
If you're a Harry Potter fan
You'll find him everywhere!

London has such history
And majesty and grace
It seems to go forever
There is so much to embrace

You know the names and places
Much too many to address
In closing, just suffice to say
It is a glorious mess!

[1] Another Bloody Church

COMPLETELY OUT OF MY TREE
Sharon A Harmon

I love trees. Trees and I have a relationship. When I was three, one of my first memories was climbing a fairly big pine tree in front of our house when I lived in Auburn, Massachusetts. I was having a great time until my brother went in and got my mother, who insisted that I come down. I had a hard time doing that. I was afraid, and not quite sure how to get down. Guess I was rescued or something.

My next vivid tree memory was in the third grade. We had moved to California, and that's when I met Palm trees. They were exotic and alluring, I couldn't wait to get up in one of them. Just like in the movies, I wanted to try my impression of a monkey. Well, it may look easy in those movies, but it's not even for an agile eight-year-old. It was impossible, you slip like crazy on that funny pineapple-type bark. Even with a running start, up a slanting palm, I couldn't get up.

Another tree I climbed in a playground in the trailer park where we lived in had a rope hanging from one branch. I got up, sat straddled on a giant limb, and unraveled the rope. By following the waves in it, I braided it up again. I went home and knew how to make braids in my hair. When I was older, I thought of the funny places you can learn skills from when I was in my rug-braiding class.

We also had a fig tree nearby where we played. It was the only fig tree I'd ever come across in my life. It was huge with wide, low branches. My brothers, I, and other neighborhood kids spent many a happy day building forts - both under and in it. I was fond of that tree even though the figs tasted terrible!

There was another tree at the same time that is forever etched in my memory. I used to climb it almost daily to the very top. I would sit perched, singing my made-up sailor songs, and anything else that came to my mind. I loved to go up there when I was lonely, pretending I was blowing around the ocean on a ship. The wind was great up there, and it was my special haven to sit and contemplate the world or ponder my problems. The top branches cradled me like the lookout mast of a ship. The world was mine from there!

I've climbed more trees than I can count, and I remember climbing one when I met my husband. I took him to a park and talked him into climbing a tree with me. He was leery at first, but he enjoyed it once I got him up there. It made him relive some boyhood memories.

A few years later I was sitting on a limb beneath a limb one of my brothers was on. He had come over to saw some branches down so my yard could get more sun. He forgot I was below him (or so he said). The branch he sawed fell onto my head. I managed to soften the blow with my hands, but I saw stars just like in the cartoons. My mother and aunt were below on the ground. What a sight! Two short fat ladies tripping over each other, poised to catch me with open arms. I somehow managed to hang on to the branch and swayed back and forth until I could gracefully descend.

That incident did not alter my love of trees. In my twenties, I went on to climb a few maples to rescue various cats. I don't know why I did it. In hindsight, I've never seen a cat skeleton in a tree.

Later on in life, I moved to Royalston, where I found some Concord grapes high in a tree near a pasture with old stone walls made by farmers. I pulled over, scrambled up the trees as best I could with a rake, caught the grapevine in the tines of my rake, and pulled them down towards me until I had access to them.

My last foray into a tree was at the age of thirty-nine. I was working with my husband and daughter on our land in a pine grove. We were trying to trim the trees of all the broken and dead lower branches. We had a ladder, so my husband suggested I could take a branch down if I got up to it on the ladder and stomped on it hard. It looked dead, but it was clear I should hang onto the healthy branch above it just in case.

I went up and stomped on it as I held onto the good branch above. I was wearing boots, jeans, and a thick jacket, but because I had no upper body strength whatsoever, down I went. Fifteen feet and I was on my way down. I remembered to keep my head up as I fell. Then, Poof! I landed in a pile of pine needles, knocking the breath out of me. When I got my breath back, my daughter was moving my legs, and my husband was moving my arms to see if they were broken. Amazingly, I was all right. All I hurt was my pride. That was the end of my tree-climbing career.

ALICE COBB
Diane Hinckley

Abel Leigh heaved the rock back into its place on the stone wall. A Confederate bullet had left him with a weakened leg, but his arms were as strong as ever. When he'd been a child standing at this wall, he'd pictured himself as a Roman soldier looking out over Hadrian's Wall in the north of England, watching for barbarians. But this was rural Massachusetts, where no Roman sandal had ever trod, and all he saw on the other side of the wall was a pasture filled with the Cobb family's flock of Merino sheep. Sometimes a real barbarian, the wild girl Alice Cobb, would appear in the distance, coming up the hill. Young Abel had been afraid of Alice Cobb and always wanted to flee when he saw her coming, but he knew she'd tell all the other children that Abel Leigh was afraid of a girl. Leering at him over the wall, she would sing, "Abel-ee, Abel-ee, going to Hell won't rid you of me." He would look around to make sure his parents couldn't hear. No decent girl ever referred to That Place.

He'd been a small, quiet boy who lived for school and what he might learn therein, which made him a target for a gang of rowdy farm boys led by Sam Cobb and his scary sister, Alice. They delighted in knocking rocks off the stone wall, then shrieking, "Abel did it! Abel did it!" though even Abel's stern father doubted his child would do such a thing. The boy sat quietly every evening while his father read to his family from the Bible and Abolitionist tracts. Abel even seemed to pay attention, which was more than could be said for his wispy sisters. Abel didn't like to see his father having to replace the heavy rocks himself, but for many years he was too small to help.

At fifteen, Abel suddenly outgrew the giantess Alice Cobb. Even so, the torment continued, but in a different way, changing as Alice changed. She still drove Miss Iggleden, the teacher, crazy with her guffaws and her noisy habit of chewing slippery elm. But now she disrupted the class in a new and involuntary way, distracting the boys with her auburn hair and healthy figure. Abel Leigh was as distracted as any other boy, and occasionally disappointed Miss Iggleden with inattention to his studies, something that had never happened in earlier years.

On Abel's way home from school, he'd often hear the patter of feet running up behind him and see clouds of dust kicked up from the road. Then Alice Cobb would be dancing by his side, laughing and singing. If anyone came by on a horse or in a cart, she would shriek something outrageous. "Of course I'll marry you, Abel, my love!" she would boom, then cackle while Abel blushed scarlet. Sometimes she would skip to the tune of her little song, "Abel-ee, Abel-ee, going to Hell won't rid you of me." As before, Abel would look around and hope that no one had heard That Word.

Abel was now big enough to replace the fallen rocks himself. Sometimes they rolled off the wall on their own, for nature's mysterious reasons, though sometimes, when Abel was in the Leigh pasture, Alice Cobb would run up as before and push at a rock, practically draping herself over the wall in her effort. Her wild hair flew from its pins. Once she danced around barefoot in the Cobbs' pasture, showing her ankles, much to Abel's horror.

Abel's father told him the whole Cobb family was crazy and that an ancestor had been hanged for witchcraft. Abel thought witchcraft might explain the torment he suffered whenever the girl came up the hill these days. On those occasions, something kept him at the wall, unable and even unwilling to flee.

Abel was out of school and working at the shoe manufactory in town when the newspaper blared the headline that the Confederates had fired on Fort Sumter. All the local youths, including the Cobb boys, signed up for the army, and in 1862, Abel joined his regiment. On the day Abel was to leave, Alice Cobb appeared at the front door, her face filled with anguish. "Abel-ee, Abel-ee," she cried before Abel raced out the door to beg her to be quiet. He didn't want his father to hear the word she was about to shriek.

Abel's regiment, 53rd Massachusetts, fought at Port Hudson in Louisiana. He saw Sam Cobb get blown apart by one of the Rebels' big guns and Sam's brother Henry shot down while trying to desert. For the rest of his life, Abel would limp from a wound he received during those hot and miserable months of battle. The Cobb family sold the sheep and talked about moving to Ohio, and before Abel got back from the military hospital, Alice went to work as a housekeeper in Petersham. Tree seedlings dotted the Cobb pasture now, a whole new set of barbarians to fight, if Abel had chosen to daydream of war, which he did not. The nightmares were enough.

On this day, as twilight closed in, Abel was ready to go inside. The rock was back in place and mosquitoes whined around his ears. The rock could have stayed on the ground. There was no longer any need for a wall. Farming no longer paid in these changing times. His family had only one cow left, and few sheep. He'd gone back to work making shoes, and never spoke at work, or anywhere else if he could avoid it. Both of his sisters had gone to work in the straw hat works. His father contented himself with the kitchen garden and household chores.

A figure appeared in the gloom, walking up the hill toward Abel: a woman dressed in black. Arriving at the Cobb side of the wall, she smiled.

"Well, Alice," said Abel, speaking for the first time in days, "I've been to Hell."

HAIKUS
Clare Kirkwood

Vernal Forage

Yearning for the glint

Of silken silver treasure

Spring pussy willows!

Orchid Glory

Five blooms in sunshine

Chartreuse dreams magenta

Pregnant glory beams!

DAFFODILS
Ed Londergan

My name is Hamilton Prescott Dunham, III, Dunnie to my family and friends.

I'd had it all; everything society admired and said was the American dream—more money than I could ever count, five mansions, a big yacht, a private jet, a large staff to take care of my every whim, to serve me as I wanted to be served, no matter how outrageous, only the best of the best of the best for me. I could afford it, so why not?

The three-year stint in prison for stock fraud gave me a lot of time to think about things. I thought that since I was richer than everyone else, I must be smarter, too. Not quite true. I slowly realized that I was miserable. No matter how much I had, it truly was never enough. I bought and sold large companies like you change socks.

I didn't think I'd be in prison for the full three years. The team of seventeen lawyers I paid $1,000 an hour to each told me they'd exhausted all legal possibilities, and I was stuck. Cheer up, they said, the time will go fast. I fired them on the spot.

See, the thing is, I inherited a big chunk of change from my grandfather, so I was never poor. I used that wealth as a foundation and built my empire with it. I'd graduated from Harvard, of course, with all the other snooty rich kids, got my MBA from Columbia and my law degree from Stanford.

I served my sentence at a federal country club prison in Yankton, South Dakota. It's located in downtown Yankton and was once a college campus. We were all white-collar criminals. There were no guards, just administrative types, dressed in off-the-rack suits, who checked on us throughout the day. It was prison on the honor system. We could play sports like racquetball and bocce ball, take art lessons, play instruments in the music room, enjoy movie nights, take online courses—in psychology, art, music, and foreign languages—and enjoy the library's 1,800 books. It's how Martha Stewart spent her time in prison.

We were able to leave the prison daily and go into the community to volunteer for two local nonprofits, Habitat for Humanity and a food kitchen serving the homeless. I didn't want to volunteer for either, but community service was part and parcel of the whole thing. I was required to put in six months total during my sentence. I became buddies with the woman who supervised me doing administrative work at Habitat. I'm ashamed to admit that, at first, I looked down on her because she wasn't well dressed and put together; her hair was messy, and her skin was sallow. She looked poor to me. I changed my attitude after a month when I learned that her husband had had a stroke, preventing him from working, and she had a child with a learning disability. They were living on her income only. She was scraping by, working full-time, and taking care of her family. I offered to give her money, but she refused. Said she needed help more than money. I called my head personal assistant—I had three—and had him contract for a home health aide to care for her husband and son starting the next day. I explained to her what I'd done before she left work. I didn't expect her to cry, but she did. She leaned into me, and I held her. A feeling unlike any other I'd ever had ran through me. She cried for what seemed like a long time as I stood there, arms around her. I'd helped someone who needed it, and what I considered almost nothing and would cost only a thousand dollars a day—I'd spent more than twice that on a pair of shoes—meant the world to her. It got me thinking about other ways to help. Seeing Habitat's difficulty getting materials and supplies to build the houses caused me to play Santa. I made an anonymous half-million-dollar donation.

One morning, I was asked to help with a crew framing a house. I'd never held a hammer, never mind pounded a nail. I watched and learned, asked questions, and took all the tips and advice I could get. It felt good to help, to give to people instead of always taking. I was slowly realizing that there's more to life than increasing earnings per share of stock or selling companies for millions in profit. That didn't excite me anymore.

The food kitchen shook me. Homeless people, smelling bad and dressed in dirty clothes, came in asking for food. Some were angry at having to ask, others stuffed themselves, quietly eating as much as they could before going out onto the streets again, and many were well-spoken and polite, saying please and thank you. These people had nothing, just the clothes on their backs and whatever they could carry. A little boy and his sister told me stories of sleeping along with their mother in doorways or cardboard boxes, of people who froze because they couldn't get to a shelter. They told me of the little camps under bridges, down by a river, and in abandoned buildings. They'd slept in a car for a while, until it was stolen. My prison was sumptuous compared to the little these people had. I'll admit that when I got back to the prison, I went into my bathroom and cried for the first time in many years. I made another half-million-dollar donation.

The day I got out of prison, I met with my personal attorney on my jet as it whisked me to my place on Lake George in Upstate New York. When I told him what I wanted to do, he was shocked and suggested that prison had had a terrible, debilitating psychological effect on me and that I could not mean what I said. I assured him I was in my right mind and meant every word. Give it all away, I said, all $750 million. Everything. Sell the mansions, jet, yacht, the companies I owned, liquidate my portfolio, and put it all to use, helping as many people as possible for as long as possible in any way. It took a year to get done, but I was adamant about it. I became more determined with each passing day to do as much good as I could before I die.

Food, clothing, shelter, medical care, and literacy were the areas I started with. Hundreds of thousands of people are better off, so great had been my wealth. Walking away from that life, which, to my knowledge, had never been done before, relieved me of a tremendous weight. Everyone I knew thought I'd gone over the edge and was beginning the slide into financial insanity. My sisters and business associates went to court to try to stop me. I told them and everyone else to shut up and mind their own business. My lawyers shook their heads and did what they were told.

I used trusts, charitable foundations, and other legal devices to ensure that my wealth was distributed in the most beneficial ways. All of the trusts and foundations will continue long after my death, which I hope won't be for many more years. After all, I'm just forty-nine. I want to enjoy this new life, to relish it, for as long as possible.

This morning, I sat on the large flat rock at the end of a long stone wall in the field below my house and gazed at the scene before me. The river near the horizon was a wide blue ribbon reflecting the clear sky's color. The rolling hills beyond it were the fuzzy green of new leaves. The wide, long field at the bottom of the slope on which I sat was before me. I gazed at sparks of color in the green field, large clumps of golden yellow daffodils waving ever so slightly in the light breeze. I stood and stretched before making my way up the hill to my home, which overlooked one of the most beautiful vistas I've ever seen. The view extended for many miles, with Mount Monadnock in the distance.

Now I have enough to know where my next meal is coming from, to keep a roof over my head and clothes on my back. I own forty acres of land, have a moderate-sized log home, and a pickup truck—presents I'd handed myself before giving everything else away. I got an iced tea and sat on the long, wide front porch. I'd never been this content, even when I was a kid. There was too much keeping up with the Joneses, although few people could actually afford to keep up with us. I thought of the poem about Boston's wealthiest families; "This is good old Boston, the home of i the bean and the cod, where the Lowells talk to the Cabots and the Cabots talk only to God."

I'd found the place I wanted to be and have been filled with hope and a joy I thought didn't exist. I found love with a good woman and a dog. My wife owns a bakery where people gather for coffee and her sumptuous baked goods. I work there every day, earning my minimum wage. Sometimes, while I'm cleaning the tables and chatting with customers, I'll stand in the corner to the side of the front door and watch her. She is happy, and I am, too. I know better than anyone else that the old adage is true: Money isn't everything.

SOFT ROCK
Michael Young

ROCK CAIRN
Tricia Knoll

A glacier in retreat dumped the boulder
between oaks and birches, but I made up
a new hierarchy with rocks from my woods
to build a cairn on the boulder. Not to point a way
or signal anything – this reverence for rocks.
I call this my creation, something I made
until I pulled my hands away and walked
to sit by a fire inside or bake brownies.

Months later, moss flourishes
on rock. Perhaps rock knows
the earth below it, what crawls and
roots, when the oak dropped
enduring leaves and an abundance
of acorns. Squirrels hauled dozens
onto the rock, chewed some to bits,
nibbled others. Their kitchen table
my hubris thought I own.

In one speck of time I rearranged,
a hierarchy created by hand
until the hand went home.
Acorns and oaks own this space,
know the rock in ways I never will,
a waiting game of generations.

STONE WALLS OF NEW ENGLAND
William Doreski

The stone walls of New England
snake through our flesh as we sleep.
The rough lichen surface abrades,
but we bleed only a bit of blue
New England blood. Refreshed
by these ordeals, we step outside.

A half-tumbled stone border lurks
in the shadows of our front yard.
Perpendicular walls divide
sheep pastures long grown over
and smirking in dappled sunlight.
But the walls that punctuate us
are those buried deep in forest

where homesteads died two hundred
years ago. The resentment
of these piled-up glacial stones
crushes through us, ancestral pride
gray with weathering and age
greater than geology suggests.

These walls still demarcate landscapes
so that we can devour them
an acre or two at a time.
The town maps account for them,
levying property tax even
on woods no hikers or hunters tramp.

The walls retain their vitality
by lying as still as possible
until sleep overcomes defenses
and we open to terrible forces
we usually mistake for stasis
eroded in place by rain.

HORSES, THEN TRACTORS
Michael Young

It was late spring, or at the very least, early summer. The weather was uninspiring. We had a weekend of lows near 30 degrees. We had a couple of days with highs in the 90's! So it went from feeling like fall to real summer. While there was some question about whether it would be a "good" day or a "bad" day, my wife was perfectly clear. The manure pile by the side of the stable had to be pushed back toward the fence, and the picnic table had to be moved - the heavy, rough-cut table.

Both projects necessitated the use of our 40 hp Koyote tractor. Of course, the tractor would not crank. As I lifted the hood and prepared to deal with the battery, I began to remember my grandfather. He grew up in the tradition that if a farmer had a broken piece of equipment, he fixed it. That's why he had a complete shop in one of the outbuildings and a black smith shop besides. I marveled at his ability to make machines work.

Maybe it was the orange of our tractor. My mind wandered lazily toward spring days, sitting on a milk crate next to Grandpa Herman, plowing, disking or planting. Spring on the farm was a time of sun growing warm. Rich, dark turned earth stretched before and behind the droning engine, with Grandpa's hands on the wheel. His tractors were a shade of orange like ours with names like Case or Allis Chalmers. He never had one of those big green John Deere's with the one-piston engines going "chug – chug – chug." There was a dizzying array of implements parked out back by the fence.

Grandpa knew the alchemy of taking seed or root and planting it in the earth so it would grow and produce a variety of crops. He had a way with hay, asparagus and mint, along with hogs, calves and cattle, both dairy and beef. Grandma had her chickens and her garden, of which we ate fresh, canned and frozen. When my mother and uncle were young, both Grandma Ida and Grandpa Herman moved up into the Cascade Mountains of Washington State to homestead with his brothers, raising beef. In an old, hand-tinted photo I have hanging on my office wall, you can see behind the longhorn Herefords, a glimpse through the evergreens of a log cabin and outbuilding that Grandpa Herman's brothers had put up. They were bachelors, so used to roughing it except there was anIndian woman who cooked for them. When Grandma arrived at Moses Meadows with two babies, things started to change.

It all would have progressed to a happy ending, and I might have inherited a ranch if it had not been for cheap imported beef flooding the market from Argentina around the time of WWI. When that happened, the bottom dropped out of the meat market and the homestead was lost.

Everyone stuck together in those days as a matter of survival, especially at harvest. Large crews of men, horses and mules labored alongside huge iron, steam-driven thrashers to take the grains of wheat from the straw. Long leather belts ran from the locomotive-looking tractor. McCormick Reapers, or some relative thereof, plied up and down the wheat fields, drawn by as many as 20 horses. As a young man, before they were married, Herman was assigned as a teamster to drive one of those long teams. He would have to start before dawn to harness up the horses so that as soon as the sunlight started drying up the dew from the wheat stalks, his team was ready to go.

Our 25-acre New England farm, with hayfield and horse paddock, surrounded by stone walls and hardwoods, is miniscule in comparison to those big spreads in the Washington wheat lands. I often picture the huge work horses pulling rude wooden stone boats to move the rocks that became walls. But the horses we have now are there mostly for decoration and the tractor to do a little work, when it starts.

I've encountered problems with the battery before, so no surprise. As I removed the grill to get at the battery and tugged at the too-short cable to the starter, I started to feel frustrated. It's times like these that I remembered Grandpa's working on a harvest crew, hitching up all those horses. I got the cable separated from the starter and freed from the bracket that kept it tight to the frame. I removed the clamp from the battery post and replaced the bolt that does the clamping. After polishing the post and inside the clamp, I prepared to put the battery back where it belonged. A shower of sparks! I am reminded that I failed to remove the ground cable from the battery, as the hot wire brushed the frame. Perhaps that was a mistake that Grandpa would not have made, or so I mused.

Yet as I put back the cables and refastened the grill in front of the battery, I gave thanks that I never had to harness up a 20-horse team before dawn.

Ah, the good old days!

MIST
Cindy Boundy

The field is still hard, but the harsh winter winds have
retreated

Making way for a gentler breath

The tall sycamores are wrapped in mottled gray and
white bark

Glinting in the thin light of the early morning
dampness

Spiked round pods dangle from the branches that reach
for the sky

Waiting to drop seeds into soft warmed earth to begin
anew

Thinking of those who are gone

Those we sought for strength and comfort

Wondering what they now know of the eternal circles

Of endings and beginnings

Wondering if somehow their spark is here

In the quiet stillness,

A light mist appears in sweeping swirls that shimmer

Through the field and settle among the stately trees

The glistening spirals bare hope and peace

WINTER MEADOW
Annette Ermini

Our Contributors

OUR FOUNDERS
AND BOARD OF DIRECTORS

Steven Michaels is the author of *Sweet Life of Mystery*, a parody of the whodunit genre. He has been featured on The Satirist website for his scintillating take on current affairs, and has written, produced, and directed over twenty plays for students at Winchester School in New Hampshire. Steve co-founded the Quabbin Quills in 2017 and was instrumental in creating the first anthology, *Time's Reservoir.* He hopes you have enjoyed his work featured in all the Quabbin Quills anthologies. Steve is thankful to all the authors who submit stories and share his writing dream.

Garrett Zecker is the publisher and co-founder of Quabbin Quills. He holds an MA in English from Fitchburg State University and an MFA in fiction from Southern New Hampshire University's Mountainview MFA. He founded Perpetual Imagination in 2004, specializing in independent releases and live events. Garrett is a writer, actor, and teacher of writing and literature. Links to his work, including other publications, full Shakespeare in the Park performances, and hundreds of book and movie reviews can be found on his blog at GarrettZecker.com.

Diane Kane is one of the original founding members of Quabbin Quill's non-profit writers' group. Kane recently released her debut novel, *I Never Called Him Pa.* Her short stories appear in several Red Penguin Publications, including her winning historical fiction piece, *Ernest Lived.* She also has multiple stories in *Monadnock Underground's* magazine both in print and online. She is the publisher and co-author of *Flash in the Can Number One,* and *Number Two, short stories to read wherever you go.* In addition, Kane writes public interest articles for *Uniquely Quabbin Magazine* and local newspapers. Kane's first children's book, *Don Gateau the Three-Legged Cat of Seborga,* is published in English, Spanish, French and Italian, and won the Purple Dragonfly Award for illustrations and Caring\/Making a Difference in 2020. Her second children's book, *Brayden the Brave Goes to the Hospital,* published April 2021, is endorsed by Boston Children's Hospital, and is helping children and families in children's hospitals across the country. Diane chases her dream of writing on the rocky shores of Maine and in the woods of rural Massachusetts. She was most recently appointed as Vice President in honor of her service to our organization.

James Thibeault has been serving as the Treasurer for Quabbin Quills for many years. When he is not trying to keep Quabbin Quills from falling apart, he is an Open Educational Resources librarian at Bentley University. He is also the author of several books, such as *Deacon's Folly*, *Michael's Black Dress*, and *Melanie and the Box*. He also has written an open textbook called *A Beginner's Guide to Storytelling*, which is available for free on Libretexts.org

Fred Gerhard is the Secretary of Quabbin Quills and the author of *Drifting to "Hello"* and *Lilacs Still Bloom in Ashburnham*. He is the 2024 poetry winner of Art on the Trails, and a 2023 winner of Poetry in the Pines. His work has appeared in many magazines, including *Anti-Heroin Chic*, *Entropy*, *Friends Journal*, *POETiCA REViEW*, and *Quibble Quarterly*. He is an editor for *Smoky Quartz*. He loves lazy afternoons on his porch with friends sharing his two passions in life: writing and dance.

BOARD OF EDITORS

In 2020, **Cecilia Januszewski** won our second place award for scholarship. She is now the proud holder of a BA in linguistic anthropology with a minor in English from Reed College. She currently lives in Portland, Oregon, where she is working on a novella tentatively titled *Headachy*, and has plans to attend library school. Cecilia graduated from Quabbin Regional High School in 2020 and worked with Quabbin Quills as an intern for the executive board. She eventually took on the role of secretary and was instrumental in helping us create our submission and editing guidelines. To this day, Cecilia continues to serve on our editorial board and is a volunteer copy editor for each of our publications.

Chele (Shell) Pedersen Smith lives in Ashburnham, Massachusetts with her husband and their bonded golden retrievers, Trixie and Kendra. You never know where writers get their ideas! A Charlie Brown chocolate bar wrapper featuring Lucy ice skating sparked the premise for Chele's hockey/skating mystery, "The Girl in the Glass," featured in this anthology. It also brought back Sherri Whitman characters from the teen mysteries she wrote in junior high and she enjoyed revisiting these imaginary friends who have sat idly waiting since the early '80s. Chele writes mystery-comedies in an assortment of genres and ages, and currently has ten books published as well as having stories and poems in previous QQ anthologies and other publications. When Chele isn't writing, she's a supermarket pharmacy tech who loves attending plays at the community college theater, and doting on her grown kiddos in Connecticut. You can find her books on Amazon and at the Creative Connections Gift & Art Gallery in Ashburnham.

Sharon A. Harmon is a freelance writer/poet and was the Poet Laureate for Royalston's 250th Anniversary. She is the author of two children's books and three poetry chapbooks. Her most recent publications were in *Wandering Roots (QQ's 2024 anthology)*, *"Make a Memory Tree" in Apartment Door Santa, Silkworm 17 Bird, The Good Old Days Magazine*, and *The Black River Death Poems*. Sharon has taught workshops on memoirs, poetry, and writing for magazines, and is an editor for Quabbin Quills and *Smoky Quartz* out of New Hampshire.

A retired community newspaper editor, **Ruth DeAmicis** is now concentrating her efforts on all the unfinished fiction piling up in the corners of her life. An urban fantasy that is quickly becoming a trilogy in the making (it's becoming entirely too large for its own britches) is eating away at her soul; but every time she picks up a piece of detritus, she finds another bit of doggerel that was meant to be a story of some sort! She has enough stuff to publish forever! She is also a cancer survivor

Diane Hinckley likes to ponder what life was like for those who lived in rural Massachusetts in earlier times. How, for example, did they react to the discovery of dinosaur footprints in the Connecticut Valley? How many people were aware of stations on the Underground Railroad in their own communities? How did they respond to changing economic times and the Civil War?

Kathy Chencharik is a freelance writer and has been published in several newspapers, magazines, and anthologies. She won the Derringer Award for best flash fiction for her short story, "The Book Signing," in *Thin Ice* (a level Best Books anthology 2010). Kathy earned numerous honorable mentions for her stories in Alfred Hitchcock's Murder Mystery magazine's Mysterious Photograph contest, and her story, "The Widow" finally won the prize in the November/December 2020 issue of the magazine.

Michael Young is the current Poet Laureate for Royalston, MA. His work has appeared in four previous Quabbin Quills anthologies as well as *Uniquely Quabbin Magazine*, and three publications: *Trout, Grit,* and a *Time for Singing*. He's currently working on his memoir, *Playing in the Weeds*. Michael enjoys fly fishing when he's not working with his wife, Pat, on their Greenfyre Farm.

OUR STUDENT SCHOLARSHIP CONTRIBUTORS

Samantha Carlson is from New Braintree and is headed off to UMass Amherst to study Biology, she plans to go to Medical School following her undergraduate degree in order to become a Psychiatrist. Writing has always been a part of her life ever since she was little and creating fun and imaginative stories to share with her friends. As she grew writing poetry became a stress reliever and a way to express herself as academics and life became more stressful, now as she heads off to college she plans to continue expressing creativity through poetry as a way to relax and unwind through the college experience.

Olly Lefsyk is a 16 year old from Massachusetts attending Athol High school. She is persueing interest in constitutional law, research, and historical studies through her classes. For her, writing is simply a creative outlet to relax with. She enjoys creating complex stories, characters, and worlds. She's always had a passion for writing, and has made silly little stories since elementary school. After working on a psychological drama novel for the last two years it is finally nearing its end, which Olly is excited to publish and share once it is finished.

Ella Figlar is a teenage poet based in Hamden, Connecticut. Her work has been previously published by TeenInk and is forthcoming in The Notebook by the Yale Justice Collaboratory. Writing since she was young, Figlar has begun to take the hobby seriously after enrolling in Educational Center For The Arts (ECA) in the creative writing department.

ABOUT OUR CONTRIBUTORS

Allan Fournier is a retired software engineer who has always enjoyed working with words. He enjoys sharing his poems and stories at local poetry and open mic nights, and has appeared in the *Beyond the Pathway, Our Wild Winds*, and *Wandering Roots* Quabbin Quills anthologies. He is still working on his first book of poems and stories. Notes about his poem: "British Landscapes" is about a trip he took to the UK in 2023 that involved a lot of driving through rolling green pasture with "Sheep all o'er the place" and "English countryside."

Amy L. Paul is a teacher, librarian, gardener, and sometime writer. She finds deep joy in life's many offerings. As a wife to a saint and a mom of two adult angels, she delights in adventure whether it be in the backyard, along a dirt road, on a page, or during a conversation with a friend. She creates wonder in everyday life.

Annette Ermini is a real estate professional with a background in award-winning marketing communications and design. She lives in the scenic North Quabbin region with her husband, Jim, and together they own a real estate agency, New England Classic Homes. Annette serves the community as a Library Trustee and is passionate about wellness, cooking, writing, and topics related to mind, body, and spirit. She can be reached at www.neclassichomes.com.

Barbara Reynolds is a poet and retired mathematics educator living in Somerville, Massachusetts. Her poems have appeared in *Pangyrus*, *Avocet*, Indolent Books: *What Rough Beast, Muddy River Poetry Review*, *Willowdown Books* anthology "Poems from The Lockdown," and "Riddled with Arrows," among others.

Barb Vosburgh was born in Massachusetts, but lived in many other places, including the Marshall Islands. She has been writing since the age of ten, although there were periods when writing was absent.

Currently, she resides in Fitchburg with her daughter and family, and loves gardening, and doing crafts with her young grandson. She fills her days with three dogs and a cat, reading, and keeping up with politics. She is working on two other writing pieces. One is about her squirrels she feeds every day and the second is a guide to gardening when you have health issues. Barb is now 77 years old and thankful she is still here and able to write. She loves the people in Quabbin Quills and is proud to be a part of it.

Brenda Anderson grew up on Johnson's Farm in Orange, Massachusetts. She was an Administration Assistant for the Orange Police Department for 36 years and then Brenda and her husband, Paul, owned Trail Head Outfitter & General Store. Now the Andersons and their beagle travel the country in an RV and explore small towns. Brenda writes about these towns on a Facebook page called Small Town Discovery. She enjoys traveling, cooking, reading and catching up with her four children living in four different states. Brenda's first book is currently in production.

Cassidy Cyr is an autistic woman, recreating the emotions she experiences through nature and photography.

Carlene M. Gadapee is a poet and teacher whose poems and critical reviews have appeared in many publications, including *English Journal, Waterwheel Review, Gyroscope Review, Smoky Quartz, Think, Allium, Vox Populi, MicroLit Almanac,* with more forthcoming. Her chapbook, *What to Keep,* will be released by Finishing Line Press in February, 2025. Carlene lives and works in northern New Hampshire.

Cindy Boundy moved to West Townsend from the Boston area and taught GED and ESOL classes in Fitchburg.

Clare Green of Warwick is an author, column writer for Uniquely Quabbin magazine, and an educator. She has been clairvoyant since childhood and offers her insights silently, or verbally when asked. Clare welcomes folks to enjoy a cup of tea while visiting her fairy cottages or walking the backyard woodland labyrinth for peace and reflection.

Clare Kirkwood's work has appeared in *Uniquely Quabbin* magazine, *Reminiscence* magazine, *Porsche 356* magazine, two *Quabbin Quills* anthologies, and has been accepted for publication in T*he Upper Room.*

Debbie Patryn is a happily retired elementary school teacher. Since retiring in 2018 she spends two to three months each year camping up and down the East Coast from Virginia to Maine. She's also had many stories published in *Southwoods Magazine* (Southwick, MA) and last year in *Quabbin Quills.* She enjoys writing about family adventures.

Ed Ahern resumed writing after forty odd years in foreign intelligence and international sales. He's had over 500 stories and poems published so far, as well as eleven books. Ed works the other side of writing at *Bewildering Stories* where he manages a posse of six review editors, and is lead editor at *Scribes Micro.*

Ed Londergan is the award-winning author of three historical fiction books: *The Devil's Elbow* and *The Long Journey Home*, covering the first and second settlements of the Brookfield area, and *Unlike Any Other*, the moving story of Bathsheba Spooner. Having written all his life, in 2016 he decided to quit his job and take a great leap of faith in himself, beginning a freelance writing business focusing primarily on the financial services industry. In 2022, he closed the business and devoted himself to writing books full-time. Londergan also teaches an annual creative writing workshop and started the writers group the Quaboag Writers Collaborative six years ago.

Elaine Maloney is an aspiring writer with chronic writer's block. "I'm just trying my best to share my inner world with others."

Heidi Larsen is a fourth-grade teacher at a small Christian Academy in Central Massachusetts. She is a storyteller and writer at heart who uses her Masters in Education to make words come to life. She is the author of *My Bible: A Daily Prayer Journal,* and her work appears in the Quabbin Quills Anthologies 2023 and 2024. She has also been featured at the New Dawn Arts Center and Creative Connections Gift and Gallery in Ashburnham.

Jayden Lindsay is a Murdock High School student whose previous three poems received honorable mention in *Wandering Roots*, the 2024 Quabbin Quills anthology scholarship contest. She also was published in the 2023 anthology, *Our Wild Winds*. She has a great deal of writing experience via school and personal work. When Jayden isn't putting poetry and prose in motion, she loves to read, draw, and dote on her dogs.

Jim Metcalf began writing as a therapeutic assignment in a grief group following the passing of his wife of 55 years. That task resulted in a published memoir and a new love of writing short stories." At 83, I didn't see a career as a writer; rather I see an enjoyable exercise of recalling memories to incorporate as short stories for family and friends."

John Grey is an Australian poet, US resident, and is recently published in *New World Writing, City Brink* and *Tenth Muse*. His latest books *Subject Matters, Between Two Fires,* and *Covert* are available through Amazon. Upcoming work is set to appear in *Hawaii Pacific Review, Amazing Stories* and *Cantos*.

Julie (Patryn) Veale-McDonald grew up in Southwick, MA and enjoyed traveling through the historic countryside of New England and the east coast while on camping adventures. She now works as a Building Enclosure Consultant and lives in Colorado with her husband and two sons and continues to camp in the western states.

J. A. McIntosh is the president of the Swift River Valley Historical Society. She is also the author of *Swift River Secrets*, a contemporary mystery set at the Society that incorporates the historical elements that lead to the creation of the Quabbin Reservoir. A retired prosecutor, Ms. McIntosh also writes the Meredith, Massachusetts crime novels, a series about imperfect people seeking justice. She is a member of the Straw Dog Writers Guild, Mystery Writers of America, and she is on the Board of Directors of Sisters in Crime New England.

Karen Durlach is a visual artist/craftsperson having made a career in the graphic arts, photography, ceramics, and other media. She writes off and on whenever the muse strikes, most often when the early dawn insists. She started reading her poems aloud at open mics after discovering the very accepting local poetry communities in Putnam, Connecticut and in Southbridge and Webster, Massachusetts. Karen's poems have appeared in the online *Virtual Poetorium* and in Nancy Weiss's column in the *Thompson Villager newspaper* during April poetry month. Three of her poems appear in the recently published anthology *Many Voices-One Stage by Slightly Off-beat Poets*.

Karen E. Wagner's works are found in the Quabbin Quills Anthologies, the Goose River Anthologies, the BOLLI Journals and in the book *Solitude, Community and Hope*. Her hobbies are current events and listening to Gregorian chant. She lives in Hudson, MA with her cat, Star.

Karen Traub is a docent at the Swift River Valley Historical Society, a regular contributor to Quabbin Quills anthologies and previously served on the QQ board. She and her husband split their time between Shutesbury and Orange.

Kathleen Rogers is a retired reading specialist who lives in Attleboro, Ma. Writing has always been a passion. Her writing has appeared in local publications and two of Quabbin Quills' anthologies. In addition to family histories and books for her grandchildren, she has one published novel, *The Loss of You*.

Kathy Bennett lived most of her life in Gardner and Templeton and now resides in Plymouth County. She enjoys an occasional inspirational bug when the mood strikes her.

Kimberly Beckham was born and raised in the Midwest but currently makes her home in the wooded areas of Central Massachusetts with her cat, shelves full of books and craft projects. She splits her time between reading and creating. Generally, her writing, both poetry and essays, offers a different perspective on common themes and everyday items people often overlook, much like her photography. She can be found on Instagram @kbeck8261 and online at http://kimberbeck.wixsite.com//throughkimseyes

Laurie Rosen divides her time between the Massachusetts coast and a home tucked into a Vermont hollow. Her poetry has appeared in *The Muddy River Poetry Review, Wandering Roots* Quabbin Quills Anthology 2024, *Gyroscope Review, Zig Zag Lit Mag, The Inquisitive Eater: a journal of The New School, One Art: a journal of poetry and elsewhere.* Laurie won first place in poetry at the 2023 Marblehead, MA Festival of the Arts.

Les Clark, finally retired, lives and writes in Hudson, MA and is a frequent contributor to the Quabbin Quills anthologies. He started writing in the third grade, delighting Ms. Wilson with the previous summer's hijinks. Now, a seasoned citizen, he has written four books and has two novels in the works: one a memoir and the other is about the travails of witches over a thousand years. The two books are not related. Les' best critic is his life partner, Irene Cunha.

Lorri Ventura is a retired special education administrator who lives in Massachusetts. Her poems have been featured in numerous anthologies, and her first full-length collection of her poetry, *Shifting the Mind's Eye*, was published in 2024. She is the recipient of three Moon Prizes, awarded by Writing in a Woman's Voice.

LuAnn Thibodeau writes a monthly article for *Worcester Pulse Magazine* and in the past year, has written articles as well as the cover stories for its sister publication- *CM Pride*. In addition, LuAnn wrote an article for *Boston Spirit Magazine* about the local young lady from Fitchburg who was a finalist in last season's *America's Got Talent*. She writes regularly on social media, with many odes and more to friends and others. \Luann is currently writing two books: one about her travel adventures, and another about the spirits who inhabit The SK Pierce Haunted Mansion in Gardner, where she is part of the tour guide team. LuAnn has recently written several articles about the international singer, Engelbert Humperdinck, for the largest English newspaper in the province of Quebec, The Suburban.

Marilynn Carter is a writer, holistic health practitioner, teacher, life coach, and co-owner of Maat Publishing, which published her three books: *No Fret Cooking, Experience the Love Light Wisdom of Reiki*; and her first book of poetry, *Doorways*. Marilynn lives with her husband,

Steve Carter, in Dover, NH, where they operate Maat Publishing (www.maatpublishing.net). For several years they hosted a live podcast called "WPM — Writing, Publishing, and Marketing" at WSCA Community Radio in Portsmouth. They have produced and participated in many writing events throughout New Hampshire.

MJ LaCroix writes essays, creative nonfiction, and children's books. Her love of writing and books began with winning a spelling bee in elementary school. The prize, one of the Nancy Drew mystery series, instilled a natural curiosity about mystery and illusion. Still drawn to wild places, LaCroix resides in north central Massachusetts and has been published in Quabbin Quills 2022 Anthology, *Cascades and Currents.*

Mary Anne Kalonas Slack's short stories have been published in the literary magazines *MUSED* and *Adelaide,* as well as in the 2023 and 2024 Quabbin Quills anthologies. Her first novel, *The Sacrificial Daughter,* was published by White River Press, Amherst, in 2024. A retired music educator, Mary Anne now dedicates time to writing and publishing, enjoying her grandchildren, traveling, and reading. You can find her at maryanneslack.com.

Melissa Dorval, an ADHD Autistic, was thrilled when her debut novel, *When You Lose Control,* was published by Spinning Monkey Press in December 2023. Prior to her novel, Dorval has seen her poems, short stories, and articles published in *The Offering, The Lowell Connector, The Shirley Volunteer, The Sixpence Society Literary Journal, The Creative Zine, The Long Dark Winter, Creative Connections,* Quabbin Quills anthologies, and *Words from The Burg.* Dorval is a proud member of The Authors Guild and co-founder of The New Dawn Writers Group in Ashburnham, Massachusetts. In 2009, Dorval graduated magna cum laude with a B.A. in Creative Writing from UMass Lowell, where best-selling author Andre Dubus III served as her mentor. When she's not writing, Dorval enjoys attending concerts with her boyfriend, reading, and cuddling cats.

Melissa Rossetti Folini is the author of *Story Times Good Enough to Eat,* an ABC-CLIO release and has had poems published in *The NH Troubadour,* several anthologies including Exeter Publishing and

Gnashing Teeth Publishing, as well as several short stories. She lives and creates in The Cradle House in New Hampshire.

Michelle Elliott is a historical fiction writer residing in Massachusetts. Her debut novel, *Divinity Undone*, was released in December 2023. When not crafting vibrant stories set in the past, Michelle enjoys spending quality time with loved ones, traveling to new destinations, and appreciating nature. She is currently working on her next work of fiction. Email Michelle to be added to her mailing list at michelle@michelleelliottwriter.com

Paula Giaquinto is retired from a career in public education and has developed a new-found passion in the joy of language through reading and writing poetry. She reads her work at local open mic events. Breaking the isolation caused during COVID restrictions and rebuilding a sense of community among neighbors, Paula collaborates with friends and community activists to share poetry with residents at Fitchburg's public and congregate housing facilities each month. Paula, along with local writer Sally Cragin (a BE PAWSitive therapy pets founder and Fitchburg City Counselor) have created a series of podcasts called Poetry Podcast with Paula and Sally.

Phyllis Cochran has been a published writer since 1990. Her inspirational stories have appeared in *Woman's World, Chicken Soup for the Soul, Focus on the Family* and other magazines, books, and newspapers. Phyllis' book, *Shades of Light: A Mother and Daughter's Pathway to God*, is a spiritual memoir published in 2006. Phyllis continues writing from the heart and teaches her great-grandchildren to write stories.

Sue Moreines is a retired child and family psychologist who enjoys writing short stories, paying it forward and supporting non-profit organizations,including Quabbin Quills. Sue and her rescue dog, Daisy, recently retired after spending 10 years volunteering as a therapy animal team with Pet Partners.

Thom Brucie's chapbook, *Apprentice Lessons*, poems which explore the dignity of labor, received the Miriam Chaikin Award in Poetry,

2024. His chapbook, *Moments Around The Campfire With A Vietnam Vet,* was named "the best chapbook of 2010" by Irene Koronas of Ibbetson Street Press and is a finalist for the 2024 American Legacy Book Award in poetry. Individual works have appeared in a variety of journals and publications, including: *DEROS, San Joaquin Review, Amaranth Journal, Editions Bibliotekos, Pacific Review, Wilderness House Literary Review,* and others.

Dr. Thomas Reed Willemain is a former academic, software entrepreneur and intelligence officer. His flash fiction has twice been nominated for a Pushcart Prize and has appeared in *Granfalloon, Hobart, Burningword Literary Journal, The Medley,* and elsewhere. He holds degrees from Princeton University and Massachusetts Institute of Technology.

Tom Anthony is a retired college administrator who has been writing most of his life. Besides writing, he has long-standing interests in biking, travel, cabinet-making, and singing.

Tricia Knoll has a special place in her heart for rocks. Her poetry appears widely in journals and nine collections, both full-length and chapbook. *One Bent Twig* collects poems about trees Knoll has loved, planted, tended, and worried about due to climate change. She is a Contributing Editor to the online journal *Verse Virtual.* Website: triciaknoll.com

William Belisle is a retired technical writer now enjoying more creative writing.

William Doreski lives in Peterborough, New Hampshire. He has taught at several colleges and universities. His most recent book of poetry is *Cloud Mountain* (2024). He has published three critical studies, including Robert Lowell's *Shifting Colors.* His essays, poetry, fiction, and reviews have appeared in various journals.

Support Our Local Sponsors!

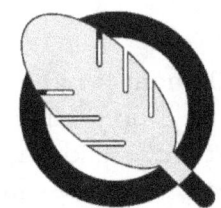

Printing yearly anthologies isn't cheap.

Thankfully, Quabbin Quills has some wonderful local sponsors to help with production costs, so please consider reaching out and supporting them!

This anthology has been brought to you

by the following generous sponsors . . .

  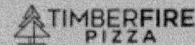

Quabbin Quills Nonprofit Writers' Group

We are so proud of all our scholarship winners over the years

Quabbin Quills 2023

Skylar Winn
Olly Lefsyk
Sophia Januszewski

Quabbin Quills 2025

Samantha Carlson
Olly Lefsyk
Anthony Salomone

Quabbin Quills 2024

Moss Moloney
Via Rose
Kassandra Santos

Quabbin Quills 2020

Aiden Needle
Cecilia Januszewski
Matthew Shepherdson

Quabbin Quills 2021

Evelyn O'Dea
Karen Vongchairueng
Mackenzie Lafreniere

Quabbin Quills 2022

Katelyn Stolberg
Jillian Mawaka
Violet Materson

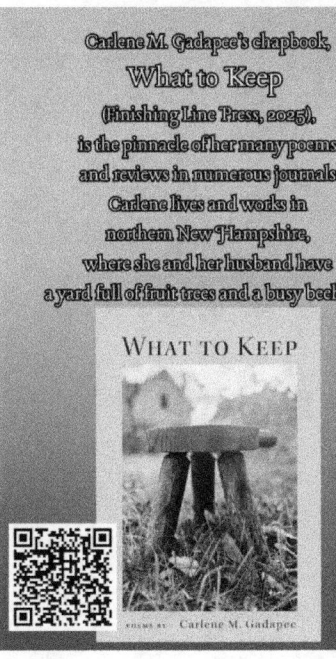

Thank You!

TO THE
QUABBIN
QUILLS
STAFF

FROM A GRATEFUL
POET

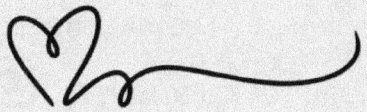

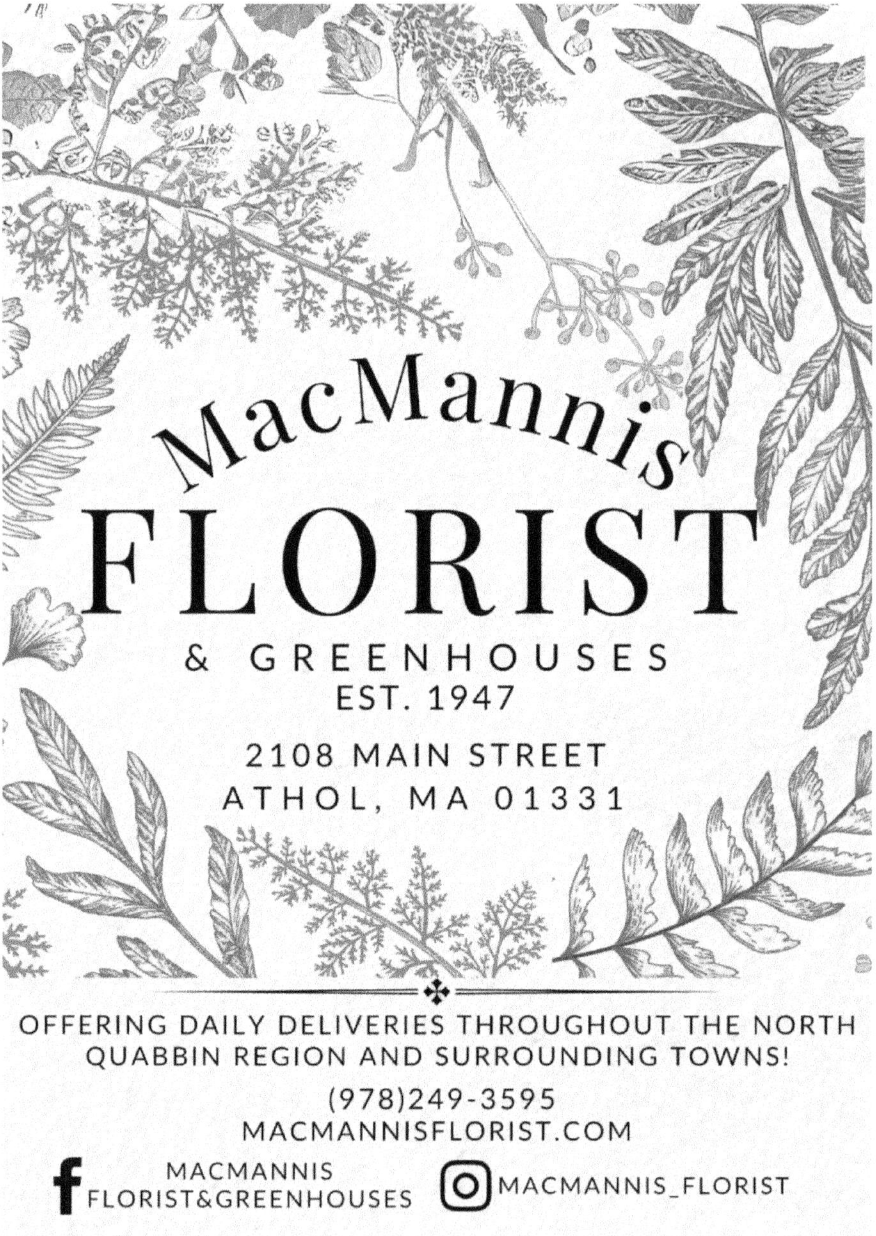

AUTHOR SERVICES
A DIVISION OF COMPASS ROSE PUBLISHING

OUR STORY

Compass Rose Publishing is a full-service book publishing house. Our Author Services team of editors, formatters, and designers come with years of experience, and they understand both the joys and challenges of self-publishing.

WHY COMPASS ROSE AUTHOR SERVICES?

Our Author Services package strikes the ideal balance, delivering a book with professional beauty and marketability, with the potential for commercial success and financial return. You retain 100% of your book's rights and royalties.

WITH YOU ALL THE WAY

We guide you through the process and provide strategies for self-marketing, designed to relieve the stress of the unknown and to equip you with the tools to effectively market your book.

SERVICES & RESOURCES

We specialize in turning manuscripts into beautiful and compelling books.

| Editing | Proofreading | Cover Design | Formatting | Uploading | Marketing |

YOUR BOOK WILL SHINE!

We provide you with the files needed to upload to your chosen distributor and help you to navigate this technical process with ease.

CONTACT

Dan Williams | 607-765-8098 | daniel.williams@compassrosepulishing.com

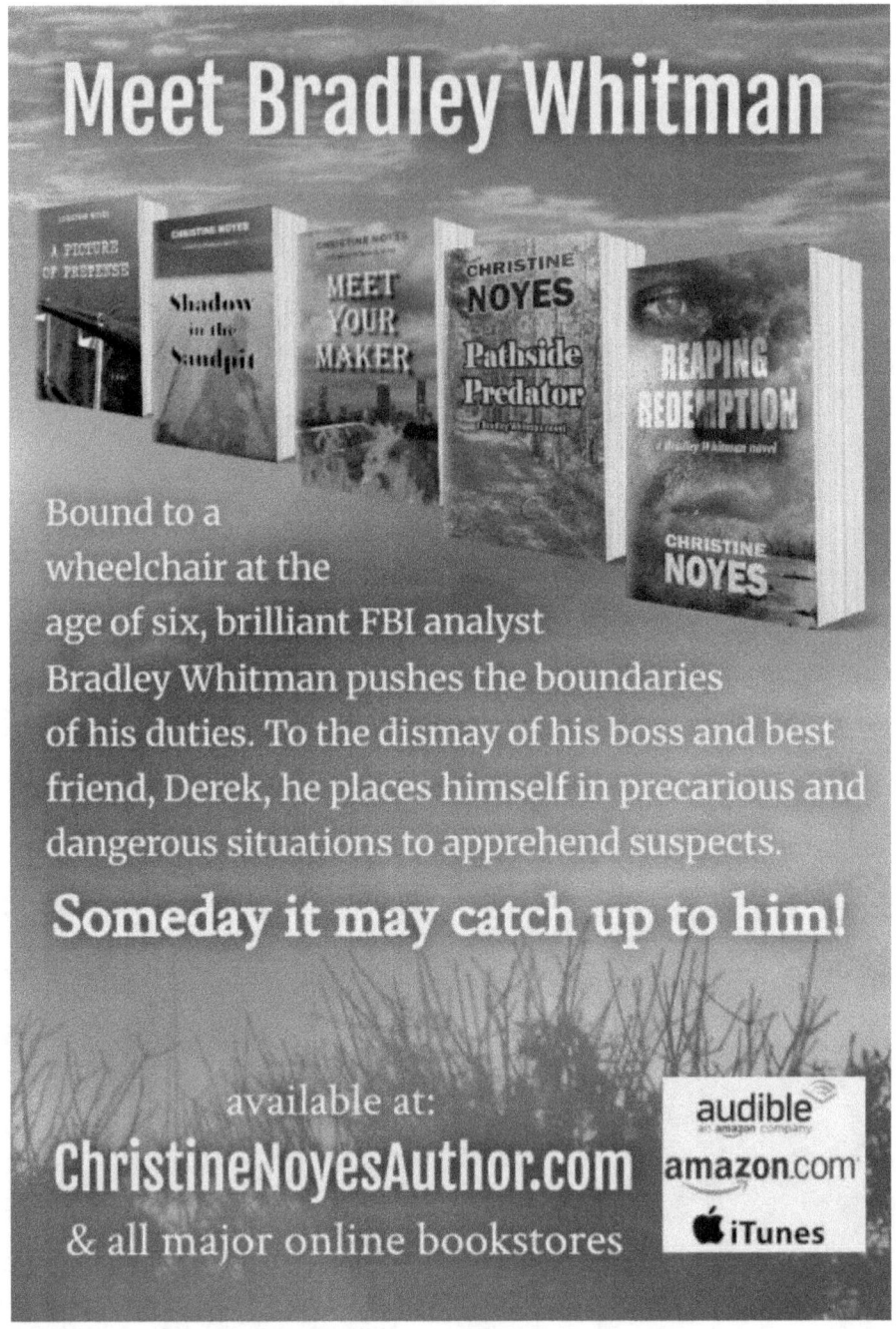

To the few and the mighty people at Quabbin Quills who help writers to succeed and give to the community through student scholarships and classroom supplies.
From a thankful author,
Jim Metcalf

We retired in 2022 and now my husband and I travel the country in an RV writing stories about small towns and unique places.
Follow us on Facebook.

Due out this year
my debut book

"Lessons From My Father"

Brenda Anderson

WITTY'S

FUNERAL HOME

158 South Main Street
Orange, MA 01364

(978) 544- 3160

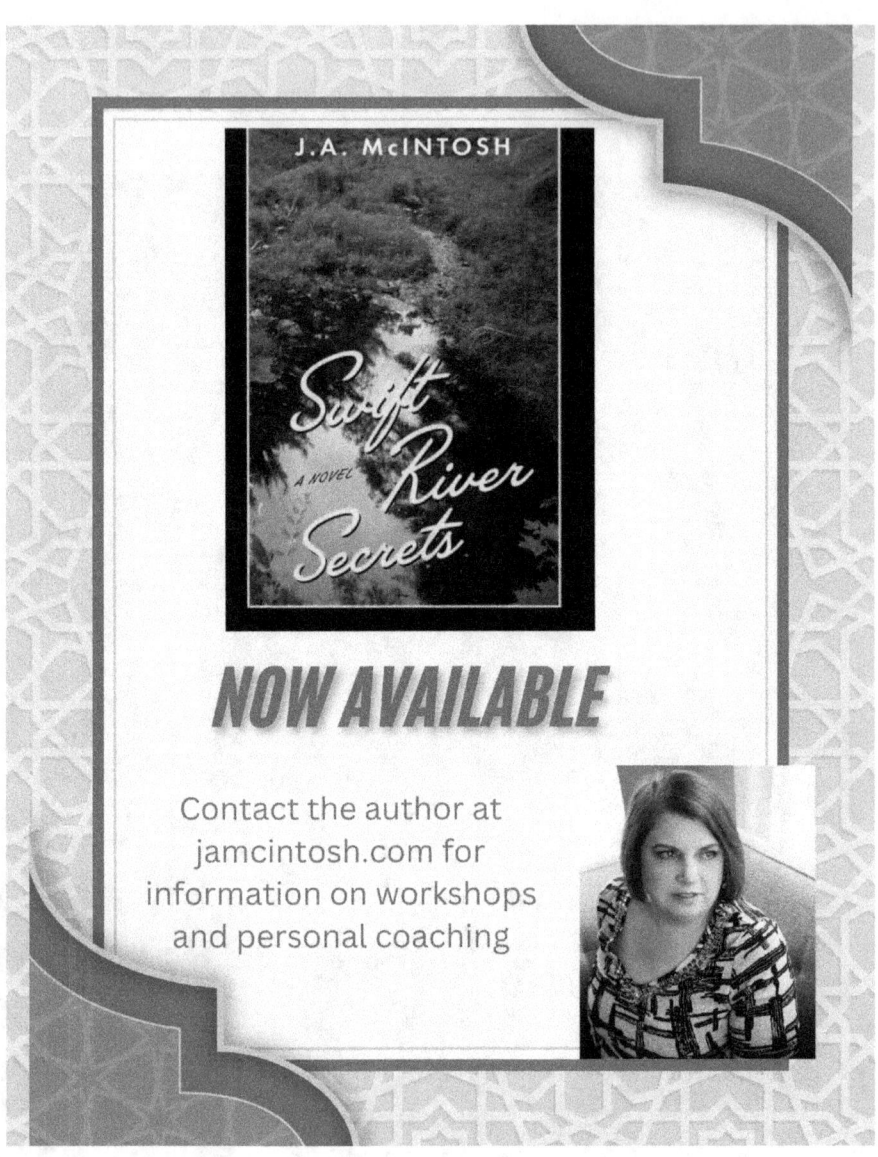

DYING IS EASY, LIVING TAKES IMAGINATION
Cassidy Cyr

www.ingramcontent.com/pod-product-compliance
Lightning Source LLC
Chambersburg PA
CBHW070106030726
47506CB00002B/615